for V.D.B.
as ever

A. L. KENNEDY

A. L. Kennedy has written ... ... one ... ... has won a host of ... ... g the Costa Book of the Year for her novel *Day*. She lives in Essex.

A. L. KENNEDY

We Are Attempting to Survive Our Time

stories

VINTAGE

1 3 5 7 9 10 8 6 4 2

Vintage is part of the Penguin Random House group of companies
whose addresses can be found at global.penguinrandomhouse.com

Penguin
Random House
UK

First published in Vintage in 2021
First published in hardback by Jonathan Cape in 2020

penguin.co.uk/vintage

A CIP catalogue record for this book is available
from the British Library

ISBN 9781529111446

Printed and bound in Great Britain by Clays Ltd, Elcograf S.p.A.

The authorised representative in the EEA is Penguin Random House
Ireland, Morrison Chambers, 32 Nassau Street, Dublin D02 YH68.

Penguin Random House is committed to a sustainable future
for our business, our readers and our planet. This book is
made from Forest Stewardship Council® certified paper.

CONTENTS

Panic Attack

You can't even touch a woman, not in the slightest. You cannot.

Ronnie is not completely happy with the crowd at King's Cross Station.

Times have changed and that's what they've changed to, is what people say.

Ronnie is thinking thoughts and does not like it. Thoughts are highly liable to make his head take turns.

No touching, is what they say.

Ronnie is not a large man, not tall. If he raises himself and stands up off his heels he makes it to five foot six, almost, and his build is sparse. He doesn't run to fat, but he doesn't precisely run to muscle, either. Still, when he walks, he seems bigger than the sum of his many parts. He sways widely with each step – not so's you'd think that he's drunk, but so as you'd definitely notice that he's there. He can't sit, or just placidly wait, or prop his shoulder in against some handy surface and be idle, because the preservation of his bigness lies in motion, his blur of expansion. His shoes are always the heaviest Doc Martens he can find and in mild disarray. They don't – *not quite* – make him look as if he's newly come from a factory floor – *God knows there are too few of them any more and the ones that are left are just full of computers and pin-clean: they've got no life* – nor might he have been winched out of a coal pit – *none of them left* – but nevertheless his feet can suggest to the world that he is a man of stamina, inhabits an industrial-grade existence. He maintains a dull finish on his toecaps, treats them with dubbin, not polish.

They are clean, I do keep clean. Ronnie's always been a tidy boy.

He has the air, the bearing, of a man who can comprehend sweat, one who can hold things the right ways and put them to craftsmanlike use. His arms maintain an extra bit of bend at the elbow and are braced out from his sides to let him occupy more space in the manner of a tiny army, invading reality.

You always know he's there. He's a one-man bridgehead, is Ronnie.

And this isn't an accident. Ronnie first started being there when he was eight, maybe nine at the latest. He's got it down pat by now and doesn't notice, not often, that his body has to make so many efforts additional to the norm, or that – *why not? They probably deserve it* – he leans in on other men during conversations, hovers a grinning breath too close. When he walks, he might be forcing his way through a clumsy gathering, a mob, while also kicking leaves up on a bumpy country path, or else hoofing the innocent schoolboy type of empty can down an alleyway.

That kind of thing.

He has this persistent imagining of himself wearing brownish, lived-and-worked-in clothes – thick cloth, simple jacket and trousers and some kind of muffler – *not a scarf, a muffler, an old-timey muffler* – and he is swinging his big boots through sweet, long grass in the mist of a meadow and heading on down from a rise towards a lane. He always knows the way.

There'd be a house at the foot of the slope, an alone and peaceful house, and it's known to me and a kid's there by the opened kitchen door and he's going to run out in a minute and hug my legs. He's that kind.

This is one of the pictures, the tiny interior movie trailers of what Ronnie wants, and he keeps it with him.

Ronnie is jigging on the spot and searching his pockets for nothings, acting out an impatience he doesn't feel, while examining an indicator board that is, as it happens, being quite evasive about his train. There is fulsome information available on a number of other trains that are scheduled to depart much later than his own: platform numbers, confirmations of timeliness, even instructions to board. His service is simply listed as existing.

But stuff changes. Add time to anything and it'll change. You can wait and get your satisfaction. That's possible.

Ronnie is so noticeable, so stridently ill at ease, that he has cleared a significant ring in the would-be passengers scattered and gaggled about him.

He spins, yet again, to study the figures, the faces behind him. He might almost be at large in a hostile landscape – clinging fronds of alien Vietcong wetness blocking his view, or expanses of dusty jihadi concealment, Rommelish foxholes ... so many enemies are available as inspiration. He frowns, his eyes staying calm while his face approaches fury. He's a quandary to those who do not know him, is Ronnie.

Not a woman – you can't – no touching.

Women are present at the station, naturally. There are women standing in the open unconcernedly on all sides, at ease in the crowds.

Women, old blokes, a priest who might be a vicar or pastor or one of those kinds of job titles, one of the Christian lot: you can't differentiate, can you? Then there's couples, kids and solo bastards who've got rucksacks. You'll always see an attitude with a rucksack, you'll always see smugness about the feats the rucksack owner could perform. And you can tell it's bollocks. You can tell that it's just a student taking home washing to his mum.

That one's fake military – he's pretending to be a squaddie on leave, but he's not, he's just a wanker with some army surplus and a fucking rucksack.

Over towards the shop which sells shit sandwiches and pots of other shit that nobody sane would eat – *like you want to eat everything mixed in a bowl; like you're a cat, or something* – over that way towards the shop there's a man with a beard and a woman beside him. The man looks uncomfortable and Ronnie wants, quite urgently, to be absolutely sure why.

Because the woman is shaking.

It's not a hipster bastard beard he's got, and not the full Gandalf I-have-mice-in-here nonsense, either. Average beard. Not a white bloke trying to show off being Muslim. Not that. The way he looks – round shoulders and a little box-set-watcher's belly – he's just slack. The beard is because he can't be bothered shaving. That's all it is. Laziness is growing right across him, springing out plain on his face. Evidence.

The woman is still shaking.

I bet he says he's got sensitive skin. Prone to shaving rash and spots.

I bet he keeps ointments round the side of the bath and is full of weaknesses and talks about them.

I bet he hasn't got a bath – shower. Mildew in the curtain and towels with no colour left in them any more. No self-respect.

I bet.

The woman is still shaking.

Ronnie does not like the man with the beard, although they haven't met and never will.

Knob.

Look at him.

Wouldn't wipe my hands on that one. Wouldn't wipe my feet. Useless.

The man is wearing beige cargo pants, slung low beneath what will surely become an ever-larger gut. He has additionally a pair of trainers with show-off, over-complicated laces and a purple T-shirt displaying what might be Japanese characters. *Something like that.* He is clearly afflicted by reading magazines of the most arsehole sort and then adjusting himself to fit the world they show him.

The woman is still shaking.

He won't know what the words on his T-shirt mean and probably they're saying, 'This dickblister bought a T-shirt and can't even read that it's calling him Dickblister.'

The man has a backpack lolling against his left shin.

Little brother of your rucksack, isn't it ...? Just as terrible, but half-hearted.

Ronnie is trying to puzzle out whether the woman beside the dickblister is a girlfriend or a wife, or has any other type of connectedness. Ronnie is almost decided. The pair are standing over-close to be only strangers.

The woman – she's still shaking.

She is slender in the way that women who shake in public tend to be. Ronnie peers at her and thinks of bones and breaking. He is aware that he shouldn't peer, because he fell asleep in his mum's garden yesterday and has cheeks and a forehead ablaze with sunburn and implied stupidity. He is a redhead. He is visibly someone who should not stay out on a clear day without hefty sunblock and a hat. But he was tired and taking it easy and his mum has these two comfy loungers on the patio and either one is an invitation to nod off.

It bloody hurts, too. All of my face hurts.

Mum laughing.

Yeah, well, I'm an idiot, aren't I? Yeah, I know ... Yeah, go on, laugh then. I didn't laugh at you when you did the same in Rhyl, though, did I? Yeah, go on ...

His mum had kept laughing while she smeared cool calamine lotion onto him and he wondered how she could get hold of such a substance. It smelled of his childhood and surely nobody made it any more and if that were the case might her supply not be out of date and ineffective?

Worked, though, didn't it? Dabbing at me like a stain. And then it felt the way a blessing ought to. Afterwards. Blessed.

The woman is now beyond shaking, undergoes deeper disturbances, spasms that rise through her body. Something seems to be lashing at her while she attempts to simply weather impacts she can't avoid. In certain moments a presence, a vile presence, might be holding her by the waist and tugging, tugging, rattling her, making her teeth meet in her head. It is forcing her to survive it and, meanwhile, her expression seems to show an almost unfathomable mix of flittering emotions: shame, weariness, grief, an angry desire to fight and an understanding of endless defeat. She is managing to stand inside an earthquake no one but Ronnie is able to see.

Only they do see. They're blanking her, but she's right here and can't be missed.

You'd think that vicar would step in, wouldn't you? That's what men of the cloth are for, isn't it, providing cups of tea and consolation? He doesn't even have a Thermos, he's not ready. Or maybe he's praying for her. With his eyes open and looking bored. Which is doing her a load of good, as we can see. What state would she be in without his assistance – on bloody fire?

The dickblister is the most discomfited by the woman. He edges away from her, then towards and then backs off and then heads in again by millimetres, observing her from the tail of his eye as he does so.

I know what you are. I recognise a bastard when I see one.

There are points when it seems that the blister might speak to her, interject, but then he says nothing, studies the train indications instead. He looks guilty.

So what did you do to her? What did you do?

Ronnie rubs the tips of his fingers against his temples, up and down and up and down. This will, he realises, leave his hair bristling, disordered and werewolfish. It's something he does; occasionally in front of the bathroom mirror. During that situation, his sink will fill with uprooted red and greying strands. He probably will go bald in a strange manner as a result. He'll start receding first above his ears.

The dickblister does finally mumble some handful of sentences at the woman, while she breathes in short animal rhythms. He does this during one of the intervals when her body is not assaulting her, betraying her, and she is tiredly still. She makes a reply and – although Ronnie can't hear what's spoken – it's clear to him the beardy blister is, in fact, a stranger to her and that she is shamed by his attention and simultaneously concentrating on stating just a few words with considerable force.

Then a station announcement breaks in.

It's someone's idea of a chirpy young nanny saying where you're meant to go – an au pair. High-income advice for high-quality children, only mass-produced and mass-dispensed and shit.

The bastard with the beard uses the smugly disembodied female noise as cover for a swift retreat. He steps surprisingly lively with his scrawny, lumpy backpack rapidly uplifted and clutched, as if it's at risk from the woman, as if she may leap after him like a puma and, in doing so, wrench his little sack away.

She is, rather, caught by another wave of shuddering, plainly hauled down by it inside herself towards somewhere harrowed and bleak.

Bastards. Everyone's a bastard – ducking their heads and avoiding.

Somebody's done something to her. And the bastards must have seen it happen. They'll have stood about and let it, too. *The bastard beardman – the bastard blister beardman – he'll have seen it and been the closest and done sod all.*

Everybody in this station would step straight over you if you were dying, I swear.

At this, the semi-benevolent female in the ceiling blares out pressing, if distorted, instructions for Ronnie's, by now delayed, departure. He doesn't absolutely want to pick up his holdall yet, though.

Can't cut and run – that wouldn't be respectable.

If you want to be a man who is respected, then you do things other people can respect. You make sure to be respectable, stay that way. That makes you a man who can respect himself and who deserves to do so. That and only that.

His substantial footwear gets heavyish, as sudden emotions push into his limbs. This may give him trouble, cause a stumble and displayed indignity, but then the woman starts up moving and he has to move, too, regardless. She's off. He has to follow. It's simple. Got to be done.

She lifts her bag, which is overstuffed and of the flimsy shopping type; jute with pinky flowers printed on it, insecure.

The sort of thing you'd give a kid, a girl, so's she can play at being housewives.

And then she pauses while the weight of it – *which can't be that much, Jesus* – while the weight of it foxes her, distorts her until she appears to be drawing up a heavy bucket from some deep well and losing, staggering.

Let yourself be lost in a railway station with a little girl's bag that's open-mouthed, that would get your stuff wet if it rains and that isn't suitable – why do that? It's like you're advertising so that robbery will happen.

'Fuck.' Ronnie had intended to think this, but instead delivers it out loud to a space near the right shoulder of a young guy in yet another lousy T-shirt, this one emblazoned with a long quotation in curly script.

Bands. You put the names of bands on T-shirts. You put what music you like on your T-shirt, so people can know who you are. And you only do that when you're a teenager and you can't give indications in other ways. It's not complicated, the T-shirt issue. Why make it complicated?

As Ronnie watches, interested, the young guy reacts to being sworn at, snaps through the first few sections of becoming outraged and maybe combative, but then sees Ronnie being Ronnie and being there, Ronnie being Ronnie and being ready, and changes his mind. Ronnie lets the milky whites of his eyes flare feistily, licks his lips, enjoying, and then nods as the bloke half stumbles back and then onto a sideways trajectory, speeding his bastardly self away, bolting as somebody bloody well ought to, if they're wearing quotes from poetry.

The woman has made it a few paces onwards and then buckled, set down her playtime bag as if it contains an impossible burden: compressed hell, a mid-Atlantic chasm, grief.

'Fuck.' This time the syllable emerges only softly and troubles no one as Ronnie's masculine boots take him forward and forward until he is only as far from the woman as he would stay from any wild animal, anything trapped. 'I'm ...'

The sound of his voice seems to hit her.

He begins again, feeling watery in his stomach. 'I'm Ronnie. Is there something wrong?'

The woman slow-turns her head, side to side, in such a way that it means both 'Yes' and 'No'. It also strongly suggests 'Go away'.

But Ronnie digs in, because he is the digging sort. 'No, but there is though, love, and it's okay and you can tell me and I'll fix it. Just spent all yesterday fixing the mother's bathroom tap and I'm not a plumber, but – you know – I have a go. I try things.' He cranes himself nearer without moving either of his feet – looks increasingly like a ski jumper leaving the slope that will take him up inside thin air: that big downward slide that looks proper mad when you see it on the telly. He also finds that his chest is jerking with these sour, inconsolable gulps of breath. It's the effort of keeping generally still, of controlling his limbs so he doesn't threaten, that's upsetting him, nothing more. He's not in bother.

And if she's hiding and down and hurt you mustn't move. You have to make noises that sound like not killing her and you hold one hand in the other so that neither one of the fingery little sods breaks out and wrecks the atmosphere of calm. Calm – that's you. Compulsory soothing.

Ronnie drives on, low-worded, aiming to produce an extremely convincing murmur. 'You can say. I don't mind. I don't mind anything, me. I'll have forgotten tomorrow. I'm a stranger. Where's the harm ...?'

Her mouth twitches and he can't help being angry that she's dressed in these many layers of fawny, blossom-spattered, thin cloth that are only ever going to tell the horrible fucking world that she's a nice soft target. She has on these halfway ballet kind of shoes that won't protect her and the bloody bag – *she bought it herself, didn't she? For herself, because it's a kid's thing and she wanted to be a happy kid getting a present* – the bloody bag and the whole of the rest of her invites every swine in London to come and have fun doing her wrong. She's broadcasting from all angles. Reckless.

Don't look weak, darling. Never. Not ever. And when you truly are weak, I mean … It's then that you can't be forgiven for letting it show. You've served yourself up. You're like a spy who's doing sabotage, in behind your own defences.

Silly cow.

'Only I think you're for the Edinburgh train and so am I and we'll miss it, if you don't come with me.'

She pauses at this.

Completely.

She's this entire stillness.

Then her mouth is overwhelmed with the shapes of crying and he turns a touch, angles himself and gently crooks just his one elbow that's closest to her out even further to be near, inviting. Then he turns his face ahead so his gaze won't intrude, gives her privacy for her decision – looks far off at the distance as if he's about to pull some sledge across the Arctic, or such, and she does, she does, she hooks her arm around and into his and lets him take a fraction of her burden.

He begins to walk her. 'What is it though you're doing great lovely what's wrong though must be something it's always something is what I find.'

The unendingness of his talking finally pushes her to interrupt. 'Panic attacks.' Her notes are a tone lower than he'd expected and something smoky in the vowels and a sense of a heat there, or heat that she might have contained in other days. 'I get I get I get them.'

'Say no more. That's a bastard that is.'

She halfway smiles at this.

'A proper bastard, darling. Yeah.'

He leads her along the platform while inconsiderates push past with rolling luggage that either trips you as they cross your path or forms little mobile roadblocks up ahead.

They want telling. They want to understand there are other people in the world besides themselves and some of them are tender.

Ronnie feels a spasm start to ricochet inside her arm and he battles to keep their progress smooth and even as a response.

Best not to talk. It's the animal stuff that's useful now, your demeanour and the way you rest your breath.

Through all of the daft bits of fabric that make up her sleeve he can feel that she's in a hot sweat. The soak of fear is on her.

Turns me over – anyone gets that frightened, they end up covered in the scent, the sick way it is. When they touch you it spreads. It'll stick on me, too. Sinks in for days, that does, curdles your skin.

She attempts to make some strange adjustment to their balance, her hand colliding with his fingers, gripping on as if she might be falling and then flinching away again in case she's annoyed him. He can taste how she's horrified.

Just like home. Just like the damp in that one little room and the smell of that bloody gas fire.

His shoulder mildly whispers against hers – an accident, accident, only an accident – and it's his turn to break a sweat in case he's made anything worse. He starts up his patter again to waylay her alarm, 'But you're okay. You're all right. It's your head, isn't it? It's your head that keeps on telling you to run off like buggery or else you should hide in a hole, but it's wrong and you can be polite about it, but you can also recommend that it should fuck right off, just do one, because it's lying. And it's being rude to you, so you can be rude back. You're okay. This is okay. You're catching a train. People do that every day. It's very all right.'

The woman attempts a full smile, or some close relative to that. Ronnie smiles back and catches her eye and the sunny patch this makes between them lasts for a couple of breaths and then the edge of weeping bangs against her, shivers her face. 'Thanks.' This appears as a cough of sound.

He rushes in again, encouraging. 'Don't mention it my pleasure or not pleasure cos it's horrible for you but I don't mind ... only ...' They are well along the platform now, level with the carriage Ronnie knows contains his seat. Ronnie always makes reservations, otherwise there's bother and uncertainty. Ronnie likes a solo seat and a little table, books early and gets cheap first class.

Not that cheap. Not that first class. It's like it was in Ordinary when I was a kid. That and free cups of tea.

Ronnie lets his longing for a seat and some peace drag through him. He halts her. 'See. Here. This is J. This is my carriage.'

She blinks at him.

'But I'll walk you up to where you are. Okay? And you remember – J. Okay? You need anything, or have any trouble, you feel bad? Then you come and you see me in J. Okay?

Or you tell someone to ask for Ronnie in J and I'll come running. Really running. Okay?'

She blinks.

'Where are you, love?'

She seems to take this existentially and blinks.

'Where is your seat?'

She stands apart from him at this. It gives him a longer view of her again.

Kiddie's bag in one hand, holding out her ticket like, like she's my daughter, like she's ...

She holds her ticket out to him, completely docile.

Bet she'd do the same thing with any stranger, hand over her door keys, bank card, christknowswhat.

The perfection of her trust in him is horrifying while he takes the ticket and finds it damp and incredibly crumpled. The woman has been fretting at it in her hand as some kind of token to ward off harms. This has made it almost illegible and no use. He frowns at it. Then he unfrowns, because her whole body reacts to the frowning by tensing in a way that aches his teeth.

For an instant he is overwhelmed by the damp, tight feel of that bastardly, tiny room they ran to, him and his mother, and the metal tang of the gas fire – the old-fashioned sort with a round, fat cylinder at the back, red and dangerous.

Ten quid a cylinder, I think it was, and the dying in your sleep from being gassed by it was for free. Me and her in the small little bed together – like two kittens that have got lost – in under nylon sheets that sparked. Head under the covers and make things go away. All of it shit – except we could sleep. In the end, we could relax enough to sleep.

What you get when you're on the run though, isn't it? All the crap to make everything worse.

He lifts his hand only very slowly and gently to rub his eyes, clean them of the bad time, and then lets his arm fall softly, no threat in him anywhere. 'All right ... E. You're in E. We'll nip along there, then.'

'No. I'm fine.'

'I can go with you.'

'No. Thanks.'

'I can do more.'

'No, thanks.' And she heads out for her carriage, nibbling at the distance with child steps in those stupid fucking slippers, with that stupid fucking bag, and he wants to have coppers go with her, armed guards. Nice ones. Kind ones. He wants.

Little Ronnie always wants what he can't get.

Her shoulders hunch higher the further she goes from him. She's expecting trouble, but doesn't stay near him where he can help.

He does want to help.

'Fuck.' He says it almost soundlessly, but he really needs to shout.

Little Ronnie always wants to shout, only he also hates shouting. Shout and you let them know they've won.

And this will be the end of the matter between him and the woman.

Even if she needs him she won't send a message, won't walk through and find him. This is the end, because she has decided that it will be and he can't do a thing to change her and how she's soft. He knows that, he does.

Ronnie climbs aboard, slots his holdall up aloft, sits in his by-itself seat and looks out of the window. A steward passes, on the way probably to fetch the first big pot of tea.

Can't keep the first class waiting – we need our beverages.

'Fuck.' It's a sound that he's heard really all his life. A present from his dad. 'Fuck.' Inheritance.

And Ronnie leans forward and sets his head against the tiny table which is only his and his breath mounts and heaves and struggles and sweat lifts on him and then trickles, crawls at the backs of his legs, makes insect shivery moves down his spine and his neck locks and his face hurts and he's making these *huff huff huff* noises that bastard strangers will notice and ponder and it seems like someone is slapping his chest and won't stop and it seems like someone is threatening murder and it seems like his mother is there in the kitchen, curled on the floor near to the sink, curled years ago on the floor in that kitchen at home and shaking, shaking, shaking and that bastard, that fucker she's married to, is gone but little Ronnie sees, feels, knows what has been done and little Ronnie knows the fucker will be back and little Ronnie knows what the whole of him wants to do about it. But what little Ronnie wants, he doesn't get. No, he doesn't get it yet, but he is full, full to sickness, with knowing. And little Ronnie lies down, straight down, like every other time before this time, and he holds her, his one and only mum, and he doesn't say a thing, not a letter, he only does what he always does which is to keep his arms around her until all the terrible stuff has passed from her and into him.

I got knowledgeable for my age.

But this is gone, is gone, long gone.

It is. It's over.

This is long gone, like that filthy, filthy, bastard.

His breath is helpless. He might have a rope bound around his chest and someone yanking on it. He might be climbing a hard mountain.

But we have nice times now, we try to. Loungers. Flowers. Sun.

These days we get to be happy.

I look at Mum and she's really happy. I can see – anyone can see – all the happiness.

The walls are peeling in at him and the floor is turning nasty – it's making him sick.

Have to keep breathing, this is me breathing, little Ronnie's breathing. And the bastard can't touch us, not now.

Ronnie's one hand is wrapped around the other and his thumbs stroking his knuckles: what his mum does when she's fretting. It means something about love and worry and love and love.

Ronnie grew up and fixed you, didn't he, Dad? Ronnie got rufty-tufty. And you never came back after that. Because you were a coward. A woman and a kid you could have a go at – not a man. Little Ronnie hurried the fuck up and got to be a man.

Heard they found you in a shitty B&B. You blue and half rotten and the stink of you covered the stink of cheap lager and piss.

And nobody cared you were dead, mate. No one came looking, not for weeks.

And you were half rotten from the start.

And when we heard you were dead – we got happier than happy.

And I'm telling you. You can do one. You can fuck off out of my head.

And Ronnie sweats and concentrates on not throwing up and showing himself as a fool to everybody. He keeps his head down. He breathes.

He hopes the shaking woman is okay. He hopes that she comes and finds him.

He would help her if she asked him. He would like that. He would love it.

He really would.

He really would.

Everybody's Pleased to See You

You have to go, you have to be there. Unless you go, you just won't understand. You'll see it's perfect for you, what you deserve.

Of course, if you're not in the know, you could walk right past and never notice. It isn't garish or demanding, quite the reverse, it's somewhere almost infinitely subtle. To the left is an old-school ironmonger's with a window full of brass. You can tell you're in a quality neighbourhood just from that. To the right is a tailor's shop full of tight dress waistcoats and mess jackets having their seams let out. They'll both let you know that you're safe, now, somewhere peaceful and permanent. And in between the two, quite ready for you, is the Salazar.

It's not a café, not a restaurant, it's there to be home, as permanent and comforting as good order and kings.

The leaded glass windows are unostentatious and give the Salazar a sacred air. You can barely glimpse the happiness inside. The paintwork is rich plum gloss. You'll take in the whole effect, the Georgian double doors, the delicate fanlight, the art deco metalwork and you'll relax. Everything will shine at you and speak of affectionate staff and the patina you only find on objects maintained at their peak for lifetimes. A modest brass plate is all that tells you where you are. You're not the type to need anything garish. Walk in just once and you'll be happy in better ways. And, naturally, if you're the Salazar kind of person, once won't be enough.

The Salazar sits near a tranquil corner. It is far from the fashionable loafers of Sloane Square, New Chelsea's ferraris and Russian minders, far from the glamour-franchised clutter of the King's Road, what has become a whorish and stupid neighbourhood. The Salazar is sacrosanct, a glorious survival of Old Chelsea, a jewel no one could ever mar, or sell.

Chelsea is not as it was. It no longer forms an interesting middle ground where life's estranged things meet. For many years, to take one example, it was possible to stroll up along Chelsea without socks in winter, to swing about in ragbag clothing, a derelict hat, and be quite unremarkable. You were simply eccentric, artistic, aristocratic, divorced, abandoned, broke, just in that kind of mood – whichever might fit. You were neither resented nor remarked upon, because you were still Chelsea no matter what. The area treated you gently, according to your merits and your needs. You weren't so terribly badly hurt by your condition, whatever it was, and really very little money could ease you by. Everybody stayed just where they should be. This allowed there to be cafés where you could breakfast off threadbare crockery of a morning, slip in past a bundled-up rock star slouched at an outside table and eyeing his milk jug like a house fire far away. That kind of establishment is now extinct. The little shops with rails of handmade clothing in British cloth, or fly-spotted books in charming heaps, the necessary late-night stores with the foods of all nations hoarded under greasy dust, the launderettes with suicide lighting – they're long gone. In spite of this, the Salazar remains to demonstrate that what is truly precious will always remain.

You'll begin your visit with a harmless ritual.

To enter push open the left-hand door. The right-hand door is always latched, as any regular would know. To be foxed by it will make you appear foolish. This is the Salazar's first way of testing visitors. So press on the left-hand fingerplate with a little more force than you'd expect: there's an elderly but mighty spring in place to shut the oak again behind you and it has to be mastered. There's a knack to the motion, which you'll acquire. In a way the Salazar is asking you to be more confident and forceful, to leave apology behind you. No outright shoving, of course, no battering. Brutality would make your fellow patrons stare. After all, the Salazar is British, has British values.

Enter in winter you'll be faced – just for an instant – by a cosy plum-coloured curtain, drawn shut on its rounded track and defending the interior from draughts. An expert hand – perhaps Claude's, perhaps Marceline's, or even old Dominic's – will deftly pull the weighted velvet aside and reveal the small gauntlet of friendliness you'll rapidly come to expect. There will be smiles, clean hands, one over the other, folded and resting on achingly white aprons. Imagine French waiters and then improve them. You will be guided gently forward and unmistakably among friends.

A talented actor I could name once said that walking into the Salazar was like an elongated exhalation of relief.

You'll be asked – probably by Marceline, or Amaranthe – if you have a reservation. There'll be no reproach if you happen not to, but it is above most other pleasures in the world to be expected at the Salazar. Then you will find yourself smoothed straight ahead and into the restaurant proper, then snugged at the table best suited to your temperament, companions and requirements.

As a new patron you will be escorted into the Salazar's genteel grove of tables, their pure cloths as stiff as justice, their settings immaculate. The bread you will be offered is crisp and warm from the oven, sweet and breathing Paris at you like the arch of a Métro entrance, for this is, inevitably, a French restaurant. We can be better than the French and yet still indulge them, it's the kind of thing that makes the world think well of us.

The aromatic wraiths of the immortal city in 1914 will surround you, dishes from La Maison d'Or, or La Vachette, or Les Frères Provençal. You will eat from a time-honoured *carte*: plump *escargots* seething in garlic, fat radishes with sea salt, *confit* of duck, rare *fromages fermiers*, *cassoulet de Toulouse* and *steaks frites* with various butters. The Salazar's *pâtisserie* would raise the great Carême from the dead, should he find such a thing convenient. This isn't cultural appropriation, this refinement, this is translation into common sense.

The brothers Chaviero, guardians of the Salazar's bakery, are *pâtissiers* of thaumaturgical skill. Their *entremets* are constructed from layers of miracles and clothed in mousses as flawless as saints' hearts, as vulnerably giving as their wounds. The glazes, the pastries, the beautifully deceiving *frutta martorana*, the soft and hard meringues, the delicately ruffled chocolate blossoms more delicate than hope – it will all be perfect. It's important, when so many are starving, to eat well, to appreciate.

You can, of course, simply appear, reservation-free. The Salazar understands the spontaneous working of your will expresses the spirit of the nation. You will be accommodated. You may also simply opt to be led *starboard*. The Salazar employs naval terms of direction as tribute to a naval race. *Starboard* lie the ox-blood leather booths and the elegant stools ranged along the exquisite Honduran mahogany bar. The booths are intimate and concealing, wink a blessing on all manner of encounters, because if we can't be free in everything we're free in nothing. The Salazar doesn't judge. The long, glistening bar top lets you feel what it would be to sip a coffee or an aperitif on the deck of a well-kept day cruiser, or perhaps a picnic boat. You will be put in mind of bright, athletic people in the 1930s, 1890s, or the other decades with real taste.

And everyone, everybody, will be pleased to see you. Mireille, Paul, Augustine, Frank – and there are others – they will truly love you, as good servants should. Once you are a regular, they will simply love you more. The Salazar understands you and what you need, it knows you feel the chill of a loveless age, of brutal changes and discourtesies.

You will feel more yourself, high on your bar stool and well informed by the Salazar's latest mirrors, said to have once reflected the Ceauşescus. The flickers and startles of the Salazar's mysteries will elate you. From the bar, Salazar staff also observe. Somewhere as special as the Salazar doesn't develop by accident; it must be tended like a garden, like a pregnant spaniel, like a new wife. If visitors weren't sometimes asked to leave it would be that much harder for anyone else to stay. Your bartender will know you better by your drinks: an unimpeachable café noisette, a champagne and fresh orange juice, a single malt with bottled Islay water, a Bellini with Italian peaches in season, Fujian peony white tea. Every choice from the magnificent selection adds to the Salazar's library of truths.

Displayed on the counter are hard-boiled eggs, and it will seem entirely reasonable to peel and eat an egg in this context, even if you might never think to elsewhere. The Salazar lifts you above the usual habits and realities. Your plate, the Victorian egg trivet, the silver cruet, the linen napkin and the tiny procedures of egg-eating are all joys and yours by right. There's nothing strange in this. The Salazar reminds you of your rights, your pride and delightful changes in your character can be established. You will be returned to your inheritance, reminded of the thefts and impositions modern life indulges. Come to the Salazar and you'll learn to resist.

The bar also expresses itself in little biscuits – both savoury and sweet – crisp as the commands of finer minds. The chefs make them with such a formidable snap that were they any thicker than a watch glass they'd break teeth. But they are whispers in your mouth. Like alibis and consciences, they melt.

Above the bar is a smoke-darkened portrait of Charles Aylward – the Founder – all whiskers and watch chain. He's our kind of person, it's unmistakable. Aside from the rather exotic ranks of bottles that stand beneath Aylward's frown like a choir, you'll find most fascinating postcards pinned in every available space. You may lack a friend for chatting, you may no longer wish to think, the Salazar foresaw this and provides the postcards to divert you. The yellowed and battered exhibits establish that for decades fond patrons have been sending back holiday views and regards to their beloved Salazar. Notable landmarks, artworks, and a choice few spicy cartoons are here to distract and delight. There are even theatrical headshots, blurrily signed in bygone years. Jean-Louis Barrault peers like a greyhound into a future containing gestures of unbearable eloquence. He is partly obscured by a bottle of coffee liqueur. Leslie Howard looks askance, his stuffy virtue curling at the edges. A heavily scuffed image shows a leather-clad quartet of musicians pouting through an especially orange-aired moment of the 1970s. They are completely unrecognisable and yet familiar as an idea. It's not that one is ignorant of popular culture, it is that one understands it and is disappointed. The band clearly failed without a trace – that's why they're here. The unsuccessful can be petted, like dogs with no pedigree, the Salazar knows that, and knows they exist to remind us that the wrong kind of people shouldn't overreach.

And the wrong kind of people are never in the Salazar.

One card shows Louis Armstrong sitting in monochrome, wearing Jazz Age evening dress and a white fez. Satchmo's face is fixed, not in the customary Thomasavuncular grin, but something like a grimace. Terror was something that men of his shade once learned to express. It was a kind of deference, apology. Slyly acquired self-confidence should always be avoided, lest the weak be confused and everyone else offended. No matter how great his talents, Mr Armstrong should not relax.

Once you know the Salazar and the Salazar knows you, it will teach you the joke about Satchmo – that the Salazar always welcomes a black face. Your sense of humour can feel at home here. And drinkers can sit and eat those eggs and look at the postcard of Pops Armstrong in his laughable tuxedo, laughable fez – and wearing his Star of David pendant – there's so much to laugh about, really. And one can feel optimistic on Armstrong's behalf. He was, after all, not murdered as an example to discourage others. He lived a natural life. His grimace was convincing and now that he's dead, he must be completely contented. There's nowhere like the Salazar for letting you feel that humanity's well arranged.

The Salazar's staff are of many nations, staff always should be. They work long hours and thrive on it, endlessly smiling. You will see them and realise they are the way that strangers always should be.

Above the booths are cheering snapshots, a military football team somewhere near Ypres, a cottage deep in woods, sportsmen scanning a Celtic wilderness in tweeds, monochrome oppidans and collegers in striped socks, kicking and wrestling in a cloud of noble body heat against a wall, two women in siren suits, tin hats tipped rakishly, as they sit and smoke daring cigarettes amid rubble. Beside them is a dashing snap of Edward VIII and Mrs Simpson. The Salazar cherishes your culture.

Peaches and cream and cornflowers: sitting inside the Salazar it's plain that nothing else has strength, or value. The Salazar can accommodate anybody, but not everyone. Some people fit more easily and comfortably in other atmospheres. That's only common sense and nature's way. Periods of temporary turmoil can feel perplexing, but inside the Salazar they don't exist and habitués can be calm in any crisis. There is a place for everyone and everyone is happier in their true place. Though the world burns, this remains.

And the Salazar's customers, they are so happy. The two women who take the back booth, for example, almost every afternoon, idling over glasses of Ensslin's masterpiece the Aviation. They are happy. The Salazar's *crème de violette* is of the finest and lends their drinks a suitably startling purple. It complements their usual colour palettes. You might take them for sisters, although they are not related. Look with intelligence and you will notice the semi-identical startled eyes, the whittled-thin noses, the arresting conformation of their lips. They don't share a mother, they share a surgeon. Their faces were both expensive on the date of purchase and if they are currently passé no one at the Salazar will say so. Their monopoly of the back booth may have been their choice, or a wise decision offered to them, perhaps by old Dominic. Their expressions – such as they manage – are less than easy for the uninitiated to decipher, but they are perfectly comprehensible between themselves. And the waiters, naturally, know exactly what the pair want. The Salazar's waiters – like angels and torturers – can see and perfectly interpret wishes, intentions and hearts.

Oh, and you should watch them when there is a birthday, a spring of romance, an anniversary. They get so excited. The staging of celebrations is refined, but meaningful. On such occasions, and, indeed, on any visit, it's easy to imagine that every staff member lives to arrive and make merry inside the Salazar – maybe readying affairs for the 8 a.m.

opening, maybe easing the last tired guests outside at 1 a.m., or so. They may be tired, but they thrive on it.

At the counter you might come across Mr Purbright. He will talk to you, being an outgoing gentleman. He will tell you it is never too early for a Manhattan and will therefore be drinking Manhattans early. He will smile and say you should call him Little Rhody, for Rhode Island. Although he will hold out his hand, you will most likely not have to shake it, because he is inaccurate with details. His glass will be refilled before he asks, so that he can seem to have been drinking only one, somehow continuous, Manhattan. The Salazar knows certain people can drink all day and nevertheless be fine and clean of heart. Others would be an immediate irritation and then dangerous and so the Salazar will never admit them.

Helena Brill, who loves dogs, or Ruaridh Cecil, or maybe old Knox, could tell you that Little Rhody is from Esher. This doesn't matter. Little Rhody is the right kind of liar, so his lies will always be benevolent. Little Rhody used to mess his wife around and tell her lies, but then her brother did something bad to him, is the story. They say that he can't have sex any more – only Manhattans. It's a wonderful story, the sort to make you feel your life is pure.

There are lots of stories. The Salazar hums and jingles with them. If you're lucky Hugo Mont will catch you – he does business in a booth most weekdays. He has a fund that gives you ten per cent. People beg him to take their money and he turns them down flat, because he doesn't need them. That's his story – that he knows how to get ten per cent. He will also recite tales from Chile: the one about the young, inexperienced student suddenly running a nation's finances, or about the Economic Miracle, or the bold general and his bolder men who defeated the forces of darkness with just strength. He will tell you the rumours of torture were untrue, although if you're soft on criminals you get chaos. Chaos is a midnight, sharky ocean that will wash away your ten per cent. Hugo is unbearably endearing when he gets that sentimental look.

The Salazar will offer you characters and help you become one. Characters are so much more reliable than friends. And they will tell you the finest stories, all of them true, all of them with a home-grown taste, eternal values familiar to our nation and an uplifting effect.

That's why you have to go, you have to be there. If you're not in the Salazar you won't hear the right stories. Someone, anyone, might tell you any story, even one about a dirty little garage near the corner of a nowhere street that burned out on a Saturday night two years ago. Its two neighbours – a dirty little newsagent and a bookmarkers – went with it. This provided an opportunity to reclaim the whole block, strip out the old apartments and remodel them into exclusive residential opportunities. At street level an old-school iron-monger's opened with a window full of brass, also a tailor's shop for upscale alterations and between them a brand-new restaurant designed to have been there forever.

Hard-hat men with nasty accents and machinery behind plywood fences – that would be too unglamorous an idea and so there's no need to have it. The Salazar's seafaring bar top, the sonorous clock that had hung above the kitchen doors since Mahon relieved the siege at Mafeking, the soup spoons, that Founder's portrait, all those postcards – they were delivered in vans over a weekend. But the Salazar combines so many things we hold so dear that it must always have been here. It's important that once you believe a thing is true you keep on believing. One mustn't be subject to change, only weak people alter, people who want to feel uncomfortable.

We can all have the Salazar and have it forever, any one of us, anyone who is a Salazar kind of person. It takes strength, but strength is rewarded among those who do it justice, those it fits. It takes courage and faith, but inside the Salazar we can feel brave and be faithful to all of the good things in life and keep out the strangeness.

So come to the Salazar. You have to come, you have to be here. Unless you come, you just won't understand. You won't see it's perfect for you, what you deserve.

Walker

I t's probably well past midnight when she wakes. *No one can tell though – up here you can't tell. The nights don't work right in the summers and in the winter it would just be dark. It would be nothing but dark.*

Feeling as calm as a stranger, she heads out from their room and into the tall sticky silence of a hotel stacked with other people's dreams. *I bet it's sex thoughts and golf and business and animals and blanks. I bet it's blanks and darks, because everybody dreams them.*

Her feet are surprised by the carpet while she navigates the hotel stairwell. She is walking to the beach.

No one needs shoes for the beach.

She thinks of this phrase being printed on a range of clothes and bags. It could perhaps be strapped across a photograph of clean families running out towards crisp surf lines, or gathering behind windbreaks to light fires and cook meats. No mention of sea levels rising. Happiness.

She's a woman who's more than capable of having a happy idea and running with it. Everything now is itself and also a code that suggests a lifestyle.

No one needs shoes for the beach.

Tom didn't notice when she left him, not a stir. He isn't a moving sleeper, always lies steady. You can tell he's not dead by the little-boy puffs of breath he lets out. He's one of the kind that sleep makes innocent. *Soft lips.*

That would not be such a good phrase to see on shop windows. Still, she appreciates his delicacy. It's quite likely he doesn't understand the way she appreciates it and that's a shame.

She watched him – Tom, who now was her husband – lift up champagne in a flute – *stupid name* – and smile at her through this thickness of afternoon light. He had kissed her and had tasted of strange light. That was two nights ago.

The first night I was tired.

Tonight was the start of the problem.

They'd been married in a barn conversion, which had sounded an odd prospect, but turned out nicely. She had expected an underlying smell of animal waste, or some other source of distaste, but everything was very clean and painted in cream and other colours which would have been called Calf's Tongue, or Tewkesbury Moss, or similar things which suggested values and aristocracy.

As the guests had walked about it had seemed they began to move more and more slowly and she wondered if this was because they were trying to act like landowners and express their ideas of languid certainty. *Or farm labourers, being exhausted. One starts being slow and then everyone does it. Your surroundings modify you and other people are surroundings.*

Tom's family had almost filled the place. They had black button eyes, which Tom didn't, but she wondered whether maybe her children would have black button eyes. She'd danced that first waltz with him thinking of button-eyed children and being watched because the watching was traditional. It was traditional to start your marriage with being in a kind of play about wives and husbands that everyone had come to see.

Her mum there, crying, endlessly crying.

She kept saying, 'I made a mistake.'

Confetti in the suitcase afterwards.

Like bacteria – you aren't aware, but you carry them with you. Bacteria, the genes for button eyes, bits of your thinking. Horseshoes and bells and a 1970s couple in silhouette, apparently dancing. Irrelevant shapes for the situation.

Two nights later and they're here. Tom remembers being happy here and why don't they just move here and isn't it great here?

Here is a Victorian hotel, a thin hotel in what used to be a spa town which the locals pronounce Nurn.

Like a creature – the Nurn. A mythical thing that turns on you. Or gives wishes – it could give you wishes, too.

Walking all the way down to the foyer makes her feel light-hearted. She passes a bedroom door and hears snoring at a level only normal for a television comedy. *I can walk barefoot anywhere I like. To the best of my knowledge, my husband doesn't snore.*

She's in a summer blouse and linen shorts and her bare feet – they'll make her look younger and summertime and carefree, a person of power. All her atmosphere will be positive for an observer.

But the long-chinned man who guards the reception desk doesn't look up at her early enough, doesn't notice her full effect as she comes down the last flight of stairs. This is disappointing. Still, she gives him the nod he might get from a regular. *I'm not sure if hotels have regulars. Before they did. In the 1920s. A single woman with an income might stay in a suite at a hotel. She would call it 'an hotel' and pay her handwritten bill monthly. Hers would be a peaceful life.*

Mine is a peaceful life.

That would be a strong thing to say.

She tries to inhabit that and pads onwards, makes the hotel's heavy doors wing out to release her. They shut themselves behind with a tired impact. She doesn't flinch.

Outside, the air is full of scents that she can't name: tree leaves and night blossoms, seaweeds, varieties of decay. But the warm dark is mostly full of the sea and how it breathes and fusses at the land. It's out there.

I didn't ask my friends to come. There were people from work. Friends are difficult. It's not that I don't have them – there just is a point when you'll run out of things you can say.

Somebody will have made jokes about the confetti. 'Look at the couple – he's grabbing her. Isn't he strangling her? They've got murder confetti. Look.' The stuff was inappropriate and people notice that.

'I made a mistake.' Mother crying with her not-button eyes. 'Lisa, I made a mistake.'

It had been a surprising thing to hear and nobody wants surprises on their wedding day.

Lisa skirts a little car park, full of dozing people carriers and hatchbacks. There's still a slight smell of hot metal about, the echo from long drives. Ahead is a wooden gate that leads onto the dunes. It's a silly little five-bar thing with a squeaking hinge, but the high mass of sounds in the air beyond it, racing in from beyond it – they lend significance.

She opened the gate and she never went back.

The flimsy wood swings, swings back, clacks and a flurrying breeze enquires against her skin. She's out.

Her feet sink into cool, dry sand and then are punished for enjoying it with subsequent labouring, wallowing slides. She can see the path curving pale between mounds of grasses and her feet like shadows, shifting on across the surprise of occasional warmths, *as if someone else has stood there and left their heat, pausing to make a decision, observe, inhale – it's impossible to know. There's no rationality in people, not at any depth. You try to fit with them and seem usual and appropriate, but it's hard.*

Through the dunes and the shoreward sand is firmer. It gleams with the weird glow of the sky, returns it. Dawn is sending up a foggy yellow gleam from below the horizon.

No one needs shoes for the beach.

Beginning to paddle in the dark fringe of the water doesn't stop her wondering when she will step accidentally on some little corpse of something. There will be softness and a crunch of bone maybe and she'll get upset. Being upset is spontaneous, you don't have to plan it.

Tom bought bottled water for the drive. That made him part of the problem which is begun by making plastic bottles out of terrible, planet-killing things and then the bottles get thrown away because of thoughtlessness and they fall in the rivers and seas and the oceans and start to be ground down into smaller and smaller pieces. Some plastic strangles creatures, some fills them up with nothing that can do them any good. But also it's ground down and ground down until it's invisible, irreversible and inside the water we put back in new bottles and then drink and so we become plastic, a bit more every time.

Tom had known she was upset about the bottle. He is intuitive. Apparently her moods press up against him like the feet of birds, or nudge him in the way a dog might – she isn't sure of how it works. They talked about plastic and how bad it was and she felt fake, because she also believed that being plastic should be advantageous. *You ought be able to borrow its characteristics, the positive ones, and therefore be stronger. It isn't ecological to think that way and so I can't explain it.*

Tom had smiled at her and put the bottle in the plastics bin at a recycling point they passed. He turned aside from their route especially to do that. And then she had thought – *When someone knows you and still marries you, it has to be a compliment. And the stupid confetti people have to be dancing, because they'd never think of doing something else. Neither one of the figures is being overpowered.*

She had felt guilty – that was a quick simple emotion – and had turned away her head from him as he drove on. She'd watched the trees and the fence posts passing.

He loves me, I can tell. He makes it clear, because he is certain.

I improvise.

It's tiring.

She kicks at the water and remembers her father, who was there at the wedding. He wore a suit with a waistcoat and a button fly, because he prefers that.

The east is getting brighter and brighter under the blue line scored across by the horizon. It's as if today's morning is up to something, or else there's a fire, a monumental fire that's rolling around the world until it meets her.

And the seashore smells of sex, the way that seashores always do – a children's place, but always adult. Or sex smells of the seashore: salt and overripe.

While she kicks it, she knows the sea is the temperature of spittle, skin, blood. It doesn't mind her.

She might be dizzy. New brides are allowed to be dizzy. They dance and their partners hold them gently, as if in an embrace. People watch and see nothing wrong.

Her father watched – in his suit with the button fly.

Away to her right, on her landward side, something metal cries out with regularity, the sound hunching and then elongating in the restless air. It must be coming from the swing park up on the green. She walked there with Tom yesterday. They ate ice cream and she watched him smiling at the sight of children being obviously happy. Naturally, whoever's playing now won't be a child. A child wouldn't be possible this late. Adults are outside and playing in the unperfected dark.

All other sounds are frail, constantly being lifted and pushed out to sea. Gulls creep across against the wind, stall into hovers and mime the shapes of calling. Their wings are bright beneath with cheats of dawn, with the colour of how the near future will be.

The swings make their little screams and she keeps on nevertheless.

I made a mistake.

She finds it hard to know what somebody might mean by that.

Apparently, she can't – even if she tests herself and tries – turn her back on the sea. *It's where things always come from, isn't it?*

If you had to, you wouldn't be able to run fast enough. You wouldn't be able to run.

The liquid blue-black Firth licks her feet, but it could mound up higher and thicken and form bodies, carve itself into actions. Everything would be very quick and horrible.

But Lisa is a dizzy new bride and very happy, she can improvise that. And her anxiety ought to aim itself at possible threats out by the swings and the sour tang of woodsmoke from some kind of prohibited fire. She should be able to position her wariness in a way that helps her. Instead she is rushing and stumbling. Any people in the dark who are observing will see her and know she is broken in some way.

The smell of burning will stay with you. It would be better if we were creatures who had an affinity with water, but we're made for burning.

She remembers the long-ago monster that would come and hang over her bed: a drowned man in ragged oilskins, dripping. The salt from his fingers would fall on her face. In the morning she wouldn't be able to say anything about him.

The first night I was tired.

Tonight was the start of the problem.

Tom would have liked this walking, she should have woken him. It would have been something for them to do together.

The first day, he was happy here, jolly and wanting ice cream.

The place barely is a town, more a big village, mainly old-fashioned and what Tom called quaint. There were not so many sights to see, but he offered her all of them: the town hall, the tea rooms, the bandstand near the swings.

The bandstand must be out there now, although she has no faith in it.

They'd watched large, older women lift up their skirts and tiptoe out to sea, the surf being kittenish around pale, swollen ankles. The women were often led about by gentle, solitary children and this made Tom nod, as if he had arranged it.

You can tell when someone is thinking of being a father – it's as obvious as a noise at night, as metal chafing against metal.

They'd sat side by side and eaten old-fashioned synthetic vanilla ice cream with red sauce and a chocolate log.

It tasted exactly the same. Just exactly the same.

And this made her heart startled and she watched her hand shaking as she held her polystyrene cup of tea. And down at the water's edge there were the children, being busy out under the sun. She poured the rest of her tea away, gently so he wouldn't notice, but he did.

They walked after that and didn't say anything she can remember now, although that seems strange and unlikely.

She'd put shells in her pockets to bring back home and slowly fill a bathroom window with proof of all the things that happen at the seaside.

I improvise.

She knows what people at the seaside are supposed to do.

A thin strand of music slips past her and she glances across to the sea wall again. At this point there's a large house set back on the brown of what must be some kind of bank. Narrow windows blaze. And along the sea wall figures wander, amble in what is clearly evening dress. The yellowed half-light makes them look like fugitives from Victorian photographs. But they are not ghosts. They were not harmed here and then compelled to come back and come back.

Laughter drifts in from an imprecise source.

There must be some party still going on, winding down. Perhaps there was a wedding and these people have stepped away from it to see tomorrow. Perhaps there were more of them, down at the swings and playing like children, but not quite.

She keeps walking.

My father with his button fly, black buttons, and he's sitting tight beside my mother while the ceremony happens in what used to be a barn.

And the venue was very much nicer than I expected.

I made a mistake.

My father with his button fly, black buttons and sitting tight beside my mother while the speeches happen and there's food, but I don't eat.

Nervous.

New brides are nervous. That's appropriate.

She keeps on walking, holding a course that never turns her back to the sea, even though it's never done her any harm.

My father with his button fly, black buttons, black button eyes and I can tell they're watching when I danced. Smiling the way that he's smiled the whole day, teeth under the black button eyes, smiling the way that he would if he knew a secret.

In the end she'll turn around, because she has to. She's married now and her husband loves her and says so and wants what husbands do.

The first night I was tired.

Tonight was the start of the problem.

And he makes little-boy sounds with his lips while he sleeps and would have been the kind of child who would carefully walk old women into the shallows and be brave on their behalf.

The first night I was tired. Tonight was my father with his button fly, black buttons, black button eyes and teeth shining under and you're with him all by yourself down behind the windbreak with the smoke smell on his hands and he takes away all of your secrets so you can't ever tell them and you have to wipe your face you can't run fast enough, you can't run.

A gull turns in the sky as if it's falling and for a moment she is quite sure it has died, died because she looked at it.

I made a mistake.

Tom, I made a mistake and I can't. He's always here and so you can't be.

When she goes back, she will have to say something.

I love you, I do love you, I always did love you, but you can't touch shit.

A person who has to improvise all the time can't be sure of what will happen.

I love you, I do love you, I always will love you. I can't make you hear a thing that would go inside you and make you different.

She can see tomorrow, but she doesn't know about it yet.

I love you.

At this moment she is on the beach and she is a walker. At this beautiful moment it's all she has to be.

Waiting in the Jesus Queue

Naturally, I rehearse a lot. No one ever gets to be spontaneous without rehearsing.

So.

I run my lines.

Well, Stephen, Conan, Jimmy, Graham, Craig, Jonathan ... Well, Stephen, we all make mistakes. I think we all make mistakes.

And that's when I'll pause, because I'll have to give the audience and viewers at home some time to think their way out of me and back into themselves. If you're experienced you know you have to do that. You need them to inhabit your point of view, while never feeling they've been forced. You want them easily thinking that shit, yeah, we all make mistakes. We are mistake-making machines when viewed from some angles. And I am a man who must be a wise man and also humble to have noticed such a thing. We all make mistakes and mine should therefore be forgiven.

Any decent human being would reach this, or else a similar, conclusion without my help. My problem, issue, focus, would be that some thinkers need a nudge to set them going along their psychological road. So I'm aiming to assist them. My interview – or, no, *interviews* – it would have to be more than one – my *interviews* will be a way to lift everyone up. They'll help me to prove who I really am and help everybody else be just a tiny bit more of a better person. There's nothing bad about that. I'll be creating a snowball of mutual aid. Together, we all rise.

I'm very grateful for so many things, but right now I'm a lot about helping. It's a kind of bedrock for me. A respon-sibility. I look back at my life – I know I'm young, still – but I look back and being there for people has been my bedrock, it's the granite in my history. You could ask my mom. Not – I mean, she's dead. Great shame she never got to see any of my success. She was loving, but she was firm. 'Help each other. We're here to help each other.' I'm sure she told me that a hundred times. A thousand. Thousands of times would be objectively true.

I practise this stuff in my head every day. Or most days. On the good days.

Discipline is important.

I think it all over silently when I'm sitting in the tub. Sometimes I'll add more hot water so I can stay in there longer and run though scenarios and not think of seeing my hands draped over the sides – some observer of my hands there and the blood stranding in pools and what's left of me drizzling out from my wrists. I never think of that. Hardly.

I piss in the kitchen sink sometimes, to be honest, because that bathroom can seem haunted by my future-spilling blood.

But not often. I mostly rehearse. It's in my blood; rehearsing. My blood which is internal and bottled safe under my skin, pumping up to the pressure required. Not that a possible script couldn't include a moment of frailty, a searing disclosure delivered with due sensitivity.

I considered ending the turmoil, the online abuse I was getting – but you have to be strong. When Chloe left me – I understand why she did that, I really do – when she left it was tough. That wasn't her fault, but being alone was …

I have experience. I can form things, shape them. An unfinished sentence creates a silence that says what words will not. You aim for that. You want your listener to fill your space with their own screaming.

You come back from the tough parts of your road by being grateful and strong. That's what the world expects of us, isn't it? You take inspiration from the great, the great sufferers: Mandela, Gandhi, that other guy …

I say this shit out loud in the bungalow's kitchenette. Something about the tiling in the bathroom means I can't talk there. I get overwhelmed. Vowels and chips of consonants bounce about off the art deco bullshit they've kept intact everywhere. When you see it from the outside, the cottage looks like a witch spelled it up out of nothing to capture kids, lure them for fattening and baking. Death under pastry. I'd call the style Tropical-Bavarian-Cannibal. It's a kind of Nazi-on-the-run-in-Argentina fantasy hybrid. But indoors, it's all hard-core deco. This is the building you'd break into during, say, August 1929, because of a reportable aroma like the stench of rotting flesh.

There's no actual stench, naturally. No one died, not here.

The living room is clean, it's warm, it has magazines on the table that are carrying this week's news. I can touch all the objects and surfaces and prove that they exist. I can smell the aftertang of Lysol sanitiser, lemon furniture polish, the sweet dust from the sheets of a newly changed bed. They look after me very nicely. As long as you can pay, no one takes an interest in what you might actually deserve.

Lack of fatalities aside, the decor provides a series of crime scene photos. No one alive belongs here. I catch myself in mirrors, just passing, sometimes and I can see that I'm out of place, as a generally still-living person. The kitchenette is just a set where terrible noir events will happen later. I warm my soup on this genuine early-twentieth-century stove that's been worried by the Great Depression, that was scared of Nazis, that whispered about dead blondes being bundled out of doors at midnight wrapped in rugs.

I haven't done anything as bad as that.

And aren't we all scared of Nazis? I know I am. I want to be part of a movement that brings unity and love back into the public discourse. Not to be an intellectual, but There. I want to be There.

I don't have to be here. I could be renting a mindless apartment with a microwave, but you have to go where you're meant to go. You have to choose appropriate backgrounds for who you are, because the wrong fucking context can seep in and colour you unclassy. Paulie arranged this place. Last thing he did for me before he left. He wasn't a rat, Paulie. He waited until my ship was deep underwater before he abandoned all our hope. I don't blame him.

He told me, 'Brent, I can't do this, not even one day longer, and I don't think that you should.' And that was so clearly poetry it made me cry.

Paulie was something amphibious like an iguana. I'm just a man, maybe.

He put me here and he was – I'm only kidding about the iguana thing – a smart type of human being – still is. And it's right that I stay with this range of decor: the crazy Bakelite fixtures and these chrome and enamel nightmares. My final companions.

Final so far.

It has been tough to stay positive, but my mother didn't raise me to give up easy. Easily.

Folksy, or not folksy …? That's a pressing question.

I have checked, yes, and no one has died in this bungalow. Only careers have died here. This hotel, of course, its whole compound, eats up the sad and infamously famous. It's like some thirsty Aztec temple asserting itself on blue Sunday mornings and bad Friday nights: rockers, starlets, jokesters and pretty-please play-actors: it swallows us.

I can feel its lips around my wrists.

That's literal, not figurative. Figurative is a word. I feel this kind of grip, like hot, wet handcuffs. I've got back pain and I figured out, maybe last Wednesday, probably then, that it's because I am bracing myself against when I get yanked forward by the wrists, pulled in and gone.

I'll maybe get found in the tub on the fateful morning and my forearms will end abruptly, just as if my hands were bitten off by like a huge-mouthed beast, a land shark,

and it will be this fun mystery for everybody – how did
I die?

That's the kind of death that's going to live forever.

You build a hotel to look like it's Frankenstein's castle,
you fill the grounds up with a village of madman cottages
and there will obviously be terrors and monsters and bloodshed – you've opened the door for that.

*Yeah, I'm at the Chateau. The Marmont. Dark times,
you pick dark places. No, it's terrific. They're great people,
really fantastic, all the staff. Attentive. They're a regiment
of shit-hot hangover cures in human form, is what I tell
them. We laugh.*

They send a girl as soon as I ask and she does the massage
thing, the real-deal, non-sexual massage thing. I never took
advantage of a woman: neither a co-star nor a member of
any crew. And don't think they didn't ask. Sex is a two-way
street, a two-way mirror, a two-way anything, because it
has to be. It's all about two directions and having to make
them meet.

I was, apart from one time, completely faithful to Chloe.
I respect and adore women.

Anyway, I don't think I can have sex any more. I may
have got religion. That rumour can go round. A rumour of
redemption.

And that wouldn't be a bad title for an autobiography,
which somebody should want.

A Rumour of Redemption – if I was offering them a
property with a name like that they'd take my hand off to
get it. Figuratively.

That masseuse? She unfolds her cream leather table and
she doesn't ask questions, doesn't talk at all, except to name

the muscle groups. She is medical, trained, and she is a pause for tenderness. You can't say human beings don't need tenderness and I'm a human being.

I don't believe in happy endings – not in any sense – and would not request one.

The masseuse would have talked – in the tabloid sense – if I'd done anything seamy. Everyone talks then, when they have the dirt on you. The bigger the news they're holding, the quicker they give it away. It's as if people are very small inside. The giving away is figurative: literally, they sell your information. The worse it is, the more they'll get. Also they make things up.

Well, they can make up that I'm devout now. I wouldn't be Christian, they're too crazy. And I can't be something controversial, or oppressive, or sexist, or warlike. Buddhist? Are they murdering anyone? Buddhist could be okay. Everyone is your mother with them, which is scary but doable and maybe even mostly true already.

While the masseuse works – she's called Deanna – I breathe in deep and dynamic so that my stomach presses tight against the table and I run my lines. It's what I've always done, plus branching out actually into writing. *From playground, to stage, to soundstage and studio* – I believe that was quoted as something I've said in reference to my career. Or else I am quoting what I read somewhere that someone else said in reference to my career. I don't recall. Or it was maybe about my life.

Well, Stephen … Studio to page … Yeah … Challenging …

Stephen Colbert is my favourite late-night host. I pick him most days at least once as the person I most want to talk with.

Well, Stephen …

I'll picture myself leaning back in the soft wide chair that's always there for guests, fully welcome in the iconic Ed Sullivan Theater – art deco again – and I'll hear him gently lead me through my showcase rehabilitation interview. He'll give me all the chances and I'll get redeemed. Stephen Colbert is the merry but moral uncle I never had. I watch his show semi-religiously – Buddhistly? – and you'd think that he owes me at least one bite-sized favour in return.

Well, Stephen, I messed up. I'm an idiot. You know the way it is, you get too tired, is one of the things. I'm doing all of this work with all of these people and I'm getting spread and spread, thinner and thinner, until, Hell, I can't believe I'm not butter.

No.

Until I really can't believe that I'm not butter.

I thought of that bit the fourth day after I got here. I'm still shaping it, but I know that if I say the butter bit correctly I will be okay. If they're with me – and I can tell when a crowd is with me – they'll at least smile. The air will warm. I won't pause after *butter* for a laugh, but if they do laugh then I'll know they are my friends. That gag is my thermometer. It will tell me if I'm too hot, or too cold. Either way, they're mine to win and I'll keep trying, although I do hope for an early success and then consolidation. I'll continue speaking beyond *butter* – their laugh will have to interrupt me – that way they'll know I'm playing straight. I'm not working them, I'm just a guy who's stressed and sorry. At heart I'm nice and I'm naturally funny and I have a good observational eye, which derives from the sensitivity I have, which is a thing that also hurts me. It won't be too hard to make that plain: I'm a man who can put his effort where it counts and portray the many layers of a real psychology. I can do my job and that's my job. I have the potential to be genuinely great.

I can't believe I'm not butter. And I'm so thin that day, I mean, how I was exactly doesn't matter – how Gary and everyone else was that day, that's what mattered – but I was thin like that top-lip sweat you get when you're in some crummy high school play and you've only got the one line, which means you can't forget it, but also, yes, you can – and that's all the chance you'll have to get it right. Four words, five words – and you truly could get all of them wrong and people think I'm like, not Jesus, but that I'm someone who can bring some kind of cure ...

I won't mention Jesus. Christians get offended if you mention Jesus, when you'd think they would always be glad if he got a namecheck.

I was brought up as a Christian, Stephen, although I've been embracing Buddhism these last months. I still believe in saints. I believe I can say that. And I can't do what a saint could do. And they have guns, the Christians. I think they have more guns than ISIS, but it doesn't make them happy. I don't know what does.

I shouldn't mention ISIS, but that's better. Or maybe weird, too religious. And all of this spiritual obsession, suddenly? I mean, I need there to be a why that justifies it. But Colbert was an altar boy so he'll understand. I should definitely work it in. Mainly humble and funny, that's what to aim for.

My audience sweet-spot is young, secular, open-minded, Internet-savvy. They don't want saints. They eat right. They currently wake up sad, but don't have guns. If the Jesus freaks come to kill them, they'll just run away. Which is the smart thing to do.

People think that I have like a superpower – like celebrity is a superpower – and that I can cure the uncurable and at times … It drowns me. Or submerges me?

The piece needs work, as does the presentation. I polish every day, but it wants a fresh eye before outsiders see it. I've always had a commitment to perfection and that's still with me. The reference to sweat is maybe ugly and I mustn't seem ugly. My main point should be that everyone hates to speak in public, address strangers and – *look, guys, you can understand and empathise, because we're all normal people here: I'm normal people …*

The point I'm making is that the way I earn a living is I have to speak in public all the time to strangers. So cut me some ever-loving slack. But polite.

There are days when none of this sounds good. And no one has called from Jimmy, or Seth, or anywhere. Not one of Stephen's people has been in touch. It is a fact that by the time you are on-screen and being a contrite soul you are already saved. While you talk about your wilderness and weep, you're already fine, you've got redeemed. They've checked. They wouldn't let you be there, stenching up the venue, if you weren't one of the saved.

Stephen, I … I get so lonely that I place classified ads just to let myself read the replies. I don't think that I could meet anybody – any lady – right now, but it's a kind of contact. I just place these various different ... It's kind of aspirational.

There isn't a single part of that I can mention.

Seeking a beautiful young lady from a good family
Who is affectionate, honest, has a sense of humour
and more ...

There are days when I stay in bed.
Stephen, there are days when I stay in bed.

The bedroom is close to a twenty-first-century space. They've made the colour palette mellow except for the one wall treatment with this Nevada-whorehouse-patterned paper behind the bed and I don't see that when I'm lying there, looking out. Only the room service people see that. They wheel the trolleys right on in when I yell where I am and the state of my day. I know that while they're explaining their range of available fruit and such, they're seeing me laid out looking like a hooker in my natural environment.

Well, Stephen, I can't believe that I'm not butter.

It's daring to be so honest and off the cuff. That could earn me points.

There are days when I'm sure Stephen's audience – our audience – will be so happy, chuckles and belly laughs on a rising gradient, that I can just riff on my theme and Stephen will be nodding and grinning at me and then breaking up himself because, *boy, in this business – we try so hard. Being delicate makes us terrific at what we do, but the pressure ...*

Because Stephen understands: we've always been this way, he and I – nervous kids pantomiming in front of couches full of staring relatives – perfecting ourselves so that we can at least entertain. Which is not nothing. It isn't being a doctor, but it leads to a kind of health.

They didn't warn me. Nobody fucking said, Paulie never said: you'll walk straight from signing autographs for the nurses and being goofy for the kids in wheelchairs – the fit ones, the not-dying ones – and you'll walk straight out of that and into this tiny little room which will have Gary in it, Gary laid out and looking like an angel, only also he's a shitshow. He's things a gross-out movie wouldn't let you see and he has forgotten this, or maybe doesn't know that he is, not terrifying, but very difficult to take and also he is expecting you to save him.

I won't mention that.

I'll talk about public speaking, while Stephen hides his mouth with his hands because he's giggling and delighted.

No, seriously ... Those high school plays ... I was in Our Town *... Patty Kowalski was watching – lord, she was a tough audience – whenever I walked on Patty looked as if she was inhaling burning hair ... And some of my life is just* Our Town *in front of Patty all the time. Hell, it's* Fiddler on the Roof *in front of Patty – I just kept coming back, would not stay down ... I was one big broke-voiced cry for help ... No, but, I am, I'm grateful. I get to do this stuff that I love. I always loved performing. Not everyone who wants to be an actor gets to and I'm thankful, only ... All work and no play and you end up freezing to death in a big maze and then you're in evening dress inside a haunted hotel forever.*

Not sure about that as an end. Maybe people don't remember *The Shining*. It may not be enough of a meme. And I'm saying I'm like the Jack Nicholson character and he's the one who went batshit crazy, tried to kill his family, hit Scatman Crothers – a completely innocent and pleasant African American – in the chest with a fucking fire axe. And Black Lives do matter. I've always thought that.

So.

I'll only try that bit if the audience is off-the-map happy already and Uncle Steve – I could maybe call him that, it would be so completely lame that it might be cool – Stephen would be doing that permissive eye contact as I talk to him – *go on, you got another minute, Tiger, kill 'em. We'll have you back in August, maybe sooner – when you've got a new movie coming out. Or that book – hey, kiddo? How about that book?*

He wouldn't interrupt while I rocked the venue. In the green room afterwards, we would shake hands. Mutual admiration would be expressed – a side no one had seen from me would have been on sweet display. Stephen is a father, he'd be protective, he'd probably give strong advice, but he'd be a friend.

Yeah, we'll have you back in August 1929 – we'll come round and get you then. We'll break in and find your body, because of the stink, and we'll raise it high. High as a corpse in August. We'll ship it on over to Broadway and let people see.

No, it could be fine.

I have to, though, explain the whole heart of the matter – the scene in the hospital. I have to find the narrative that works, my explanation, and that's been tough.

I rise to a challenge, though, Stephen.

I rise to them over and over – it's not as if life hasn't all been a fucking challenge. I mean, how many people manage to parlay a supporting role in a stinking kids' TV show into being a real live – currently – leading man? Mainstream and demanding indy roles. How many? Tell me. Not many – that's the answer. Motherhumping few.

Pardon me, Stephen, but very few.

I can carry a movie. My name. It could do that. We had a couple of scripts in the works. I have a production company. I was going to front a series of ads for a children's charity.

Yeah.

That.

They cancelled.

But people can still remember I had status.

Status is like sliding down a razor blade – the harder and faster you go, well, the deeper you get cut.

They repeat my show, that lousy old show. My problem is kids see it and they think it's now. I left it for good and it folded without me. My absence hit it hard, because I had come to be a favourite, an essential, and also no one was a kid any more – not me, not anyone among the central characters, not even close – so the producers would have had to recast, or change everything: send us to college, give us jobs, adult jobs, get us married, give us mortgages, erectile dysfunction, razor blades – impossible shit like that.

They just cancelled it instead. The seventh series of The Chadwicks Got Magics *was the last.*

It should have faded.

But it fucking doesn't. It does not. It never dies. All the worst shit never dies.

They show it in Kazakhstan. Kazakhstan. It keeps on and on repeating and the kids watch it and they think that I am still a kid myself and some kids get sick and they get hurt and they have messed-up, rare conditions and catch terrible diseases and they write to my agent, or they call, or they email. They hand-make me cards with energy no one responsible should let them use. And they expect me to do something. Or else their families, their schools, their priests, their pastors – God knows and it doesn't matter – there are just too many people who keep having this bright idea that somebody famous can turn up like a whistled rescue dog and make the worst thing in the world be better.

Steve, Uncle Steve, I send photos and autographs, but that isn't enough. Letters aren't enough. They want me to be there, wherever they are: the sick ones, the dying ones. The whole world, Steve – it's this howling kiddie Jesus queue and they're waiting in line and they want me, 24/7.

Not an acceptable way to say it.

What is acceptable, though? What could be acceptable about walking into a bright, bright, tiny room and looking straight into a face – Gary's face – and knowing he's so fucked up he is *gone*?

I had like an unstoppable reaction when I saw him, an instinct that I couldn't help kicked in, it made me, against my will, need to just get out of there.

It was a fight or flight situation.

And I don't think he even knew me or gave a shit about who I am. I don't think he ever could show a reaction, not like a person would. There were monitors and cables, tubes, liquids and there was this smell – it wasn't possible to be there.

I couldn't be there. I would have needed training and I have no training.

I ran out of the room, because I was going to throw up. I could hardly stay and hurl at a kid who is dying and who maybe possibly liked my show and maybe possibly knew who I am and cared. I couldn't do that in front of his parents.

I don't know what they were thinking and it was their fault, for sure, that I was there. There is some shared responsibility and guilt in the situation and that has never been acknowledged and I'm too much of a decent person to say, in fact.

Being frank, their only son was dying and they wanted to score some fame.

I had to run.

Maybe they thought I could truly help and that the fame would help. People always imagine fame will help.

I don't know, Stephen, I just ran. I have regretted it ever since, every day. I promise you.

I went back the following morning and it was sad, it was tragic, that he had died overnight and that people were dealing with the new fact of his absence. They were desperate and angry and a bunch of other stuff. They frightened me, if I'm being wholly truthful. I have never mentioned that online.

And while they were yelling at me, they said that he smiled when he saw me and was crying after I'd gone. I ruined his last evening, is what they told me.

I do not believe that he smiled. I was not in any way aware of smiling. He was not so much of a freak that I wouldn't have noticed him smiling.

I wholeheartedly respect Gary's parents for the efforts that they made, sharing his struggle and so many just bleak and harsh times. There's because of legal stuff, there are things I can't say. But my heart breaks for them and I offer them my thoughts and prayers.

And I wish I had not been unwell on the day in question – the day of my first visit – and that I had not been taking unfamiliar medication. I wish I had not been tired and unwell and disoriented. I wish the statements I made at the time had been more coherent and precise.

I am a young man and do not know anything about death. I have no experience.

I sit in the lounge after the cleaner goes and before the masseuse and I make up better situations for myself – like if I'd had a pet and the pet had died. Or if I'd had a few pets and deaths. If Stephen was really my uncle he'd have bought me pets, because of the unconditional love they provide and that essential experience of mortality.

My father didn't have any brothers, though – nor my mother. And now I'm considering my parents, they can burn in hell. They can take their in-depth exclusives and their 'we tried our poor best' and every true and shocking story of a wayward, tormented, troubled whateverthefuck and they can hold it tight while they burn.

They make more money out of me than I do.

Stephen, as you know, my father and I have never seen eye to eye. It is a troublesome situation. Let's just say that if I had been dying, the piece of shit would not have broken stride as he headed for his latest sophomore girlfriend. The faculty dumped him. And my mother is not unfamiliar with Quaaludes, Adderall, and who knows anything except they deserve each other and I did not deserve them.

No. Mustn't sound sour.

We have to go high when they go low.

No jokes about Dad's support for the student body.

Somebody like Stephen would just have been proud of me. That's all. A good father and mother would have stood on their clean little stoop and been arm in arm and puzzled by anything untoward. They'd have said I was a fine, mature, smart and justifiably wealthy young man, only twenty-five years old, but often incredibly mature, very attractive, self-confident, someone who neither smokes nor drinks, and has a good sense of humour.

It would make me proud.

On the days when I don't get out of bed, The Latest Statement From His Parents gives me hope.

I self-medicate a little – I'd say it's a little – sleeping is tricky, as is eating and thinking some thoughts – but I am mainly comforted by the knowledge that my work has been appreciated by my many loyal fans and the fact that young men can behave unwisely, especially when they are burdened beyond their years and confronted unexpectedly by great shocks.

Fame is a shock. Fame is a permanent panic attack on a red carpet.

Everyone knows that young men have periods of weakness and I am a young man. What happened was inevitable and part of nature. Any decent human being would reach this conclusion and give me the benefit of their doubt.

This is what I believe.

Even in the bath I can sometimes believe it.

I also say to myself, some evenings, mornings, in loose hours, 'Brent, I can't do this, not even one day longer, and I don't think that you should.' I can imitate Paulie's voice uncannily well, because I have this great ear for voices, and as I speak it's almost as if he's right here in the room, close beside me and ready to help.

The poetry of that always makes me cry.

Unanswered

Twice I've lived in a bombsite house and I've known it both the times. That's even though no one had told me, because people don't. A person doesn't say to another person that the house they are trying to sell is a real house now, but some other house in some other shape was here before and some breath you'd have taken in it, safe under its roof, would have felt just fine, but the next would have burned and been torn up into spatters. Who would say that? A bomb is a detail that no one can want.

A new construction on a bombsite is also a halfway resurrection. Who'd want to hear that? When you set your foundations down into shocked earth, earth that remembers, then nothing you build will be new, not absolutely. The homes that you make will be all tangled up in these rags and embers of previous life. They'll most often be the kind of wrong place you'll offer to the poor.

Poor in London, or course, can mean anything, can't it? Millionaire London, all that money pouring upwards and away from people, but still rocking from old bombs.

A home is supposed to hold people not investments. The good ones are built to be a human space, something that learns to have a human nature. And what human would want to end up being halfway resurrected, kicked out of the grave? Clothes all rotted and earth in your mouth – you'd understand you were a monster. You'd look down at your hands and you'd be disgusted.

I don't know about Heaven, and the people who do say very conflicting things about it, but I think I'd want the dead to have nothingness and quiet, a rest. Somewhere eternal – you couldn't make sense of that, could you? You'd go mad. And poor Lazarus, rotten-fingered, up and out and keeping on in some terrible state – how would you stand it?

So those two places where I lived, they were Lazarus houses. Much later I checked up the records, got the bomb maps, but I already knew they weren't right, I could tell.

I believe all the Lazarus buildings are much the same: they tremble when it's dark. It won't be every night, but in the end I'm bound to feel them. The shaking's not absolutely in the air, or in the floor, or in the door frames, it's not absolutely any bloody where – but it's there. It almost feels like an animal shivering against you.

This city isn't quite where I began, but I do understand it, and underneath the grind that's London, the anthill motion, there's still the shiver from thousands of homes that remember blood. Whenever the sun sets, any amount of them echo and rock. Wars never go away, I knew that even when I was little – from 1949, 1950, when I was about five or six. I'd dream of high fires and broken houses. The cement and the mortar, the baked-alive clay in London's bricks would catch me inside their memories and I'd open my eyes to the dark. The shakes that I'd dreamed would still be there, real as real, against my skin. I was shut inside them.

And what would you do, alone there with the bomb ghosts, the side wall of your building braced with timbers and a nightmare in the gap next door where there's no more house? What I did was get up and run away.

I'd never be clear on the details, but I'd end up in the streets, sloping along and out of breath. I'd be wearing my pyjamas underneath a coat, bare feet and this coat that was cut down from a neighbour's older, taller boy and still too big. It was brownish and scratched me. I must have looked like a Displaced Person, still on the move and nobody with him, tiny blond kid with blue eyes to make you notice. I was happy, though, happy wandering. I'd stay on the move until dawn would turn me back, wash me clear of the past so I could walk back home.

Used to drive my mother crazy. She'd think that she ought to be able to make herself sleep lightly and notice when I tried to slip away. I made her imagine she was a bad mother and that wasn't true in any way.

Not that she was my mother. She was someone who went up to Hampstead and into this big old house where a Socialist lady was making a hobby of saving children. Being blond with the blue eyes, I might have drawn attention. Otherwise, one baby's much like another, I'd guess. For whatever reason Mum saw me and met me and then she decided to love me, when I'd never been a part of her and so she didn't have an obligation. I've always thought that was a wonderful thing, wasn't it? My father went along with what she wanted and, by the time I was old enough to notice, he loved me, too.

I naturally didn't want to hurt my parents, but I couldn't help going out on the march at night. As I grew older, in fact, I'd look forward to the next compulsion. Half asleep, I'd still turn the lock, draw the bolt, move aside the chairs and boxes they'd put in my way, whatever was stopping me opening the front door.

Moving free inside a great, busy city that's turned tranquil – there are few things as lovely. The pavement's yours, the road's yours, the silence and the sky and the taste of the secret air – they're yours. You're an aristocrat, but better. Anyone you meet's a brother or a sister in this progress that you're making and you feel struck up joyful like a tune. Any window showing light is your secret. Any figure at the glass is a beautiful mystery, while you navigate your solitude. They seem precious, these shadow people, and you're out among them and maybe precious, too.

As I got older I used to think the right face looking down at me from the right window would be my girl, would just tip out my heart and drink me like warm water with one glance. I was a romantic.

If I consider it now: a kid on his own, on her own, and outside in darkness – that's never safe, is it? But I felt at the time that I was untouchable. The city shook me out to meet it at a time when it could enjoy showing me itself and, of course, I assumed it would always look after me. I never even cut my feet and that's just unlikely, isn't it?

A lot of the streets were still rubble and craters from after the Blitz. People forget how long it took to rebuild things. Various kinds of shambles were normal to everyone then: the disappeared addresses, the wooden beams propping us up and the solitary walls still standing unsupported. There were long stretches of absence: no more parlours, no more rag rugs, no more floorboards, no more ornaments, no clocks, no mantelpieces underneath them. After nightfall every darkness was so deep it seemed solid. In daylight you would see the scars on burnt joists and what had become of the paper in strangers' rooms, the repeating patterns worked on by the weather, peeling away. This didn't seem a peculiar setting for a childhood. There always are children somewhere who'd recognise it, versions of it, and England had come round to have its turn. I suppose the broken walls could have toppled and killed me as I passed. That was a risk. And there were abandoned shelters waiting, with the wet and the black and the cold frogs in their mouths, and no one could tell what else was hiding in them. I'd hear stories, which I didn't understand, about knives and wallets and sliced-away clothes, being chucked in the lousy shelter water after, being left for Dead.

People would say that quite often – left for Dead.

I thought Dead was the name for someone and he'd come round and just take you, if you didn't watch. Dead was waiting. Dead wore tall boots and a hat with a peak and he stole away people, had eternity to fill. Still, I knew he wouldn't get me in the nights while I was walking, they were blessed. I was out letting London tell me the ways it was hurt and so it would protect me.

I'd overhear stories about Death inside broken buildings and the streets where the lamps weren't lit. There was talk about sex which made it always seem like a wrong-headed dog you should keep on a chain: appetite and tearing and a bad kind of speed. At that age, though, I didn't feel offended on behalf of love and how it can show itself gently. I didn't understand.

And nothing bad did happen, not to me. While I roamed about I was permanently lucky.

I'd get found, unscathed and on my slow way home, by this policeman, or that policeman, a neighbour, a milkman, another policeman. The policeman who met me first was gentle and had a uniform that smelled of mothballs and a son who was younger than me. He had been at Dunkirk and sunk to his chest in lousy water for hours upon hours. He'd been close to Dead. This seems now a strange thing to tell me about, while we walked side by side and the sparrows and the starlings all woke up exactly as we passed them, it seemed, and the dawn light sparked the colour of the bombweed and made it so violetpink and purple and so strong that I could taste it. I had to shout above how bright it was and maybe so did he as he let me hear what must have been the story most on his mind. The name for bombweed is rosebay willowherb at present, because people have forgotten what it's for. It's one of the things that grows right after bombs: like poppies and like oleander.

The late-August heat started rising with the dust as we passed: a barefooted boy in a coat he didn't need and a policeman and the glimmer up aloft of the early, linty, little seeds of bombweed that drifted like unnatural snow.

Sometimes bomb ghosts gave me lovely mornings.

On my very first bomb morning, Mum hadn't discovered I'd got out. Why would anyone think that I might try to? She'd woken and stirred herself, put the water on for tea and was cooking my dad breakfast. Next she'd have started on breakfast for me, she'd have called and expected my answer. Dad was cleaning his shoes because he liked them regulation proper on behalf of the Royal Electrical and Mechanical Engineers, although they no longer took an interest in his footwear. He cared on their behalf and buffed and polished meticulously, leaned over the front and back pages of the *Daily Worker*, which he always spread out flat on the lino to catch any bits. He'd work until the leather was parade-ground smart and sometimes he'd also be reading the paper and nodding a bit, or sometimes he'd be ideologically affronted – especially after Hungary in '56. He'd swipe his brush across the words he disagreed with, black them out like a censor.

That was the start of most days for me: his brushes making whispers and the smell of polish and my mother humming her way through no particular song and breathing in the taste of frying bread, or bacon, or else there'd be the spitting of an egg. I think my mum knew somebody with hens. I assumed that our situation and how it was perfect would be eternal – like a bearable Paradise – and I was pleased by the way that our big yellow kettle whistled.

When the constable led me home, back to our flat, I couldn't explain why I'd gone out of Paradise. How would anyone? I couldn't tell anybody about the bombs. My mother grabbed my shoulders and said nothing while two men from the forces looked down at each other's toecaps and decided they were friends. They swapped handshakes and thank yous and Mum's fingertips were sore against my collarbones. And then there were more thank yous and goodbyes, Mum's face gone white with keeping quiet, and my policeman told me that I was a sturdy, hardy chap, but he hoped that he wouldn't see me out at night again.

He did, though. I was a repeat offender.

And after he'd gone my mum did some of her best shouting. She was louder than my dad and I had ever known her. We kept our heads down.

I didn't want to make her fierce, or to upset her. She didn't want to upset me. It was only that she needed me to be different, but I couldn't. I was myself, the one she picked.

Every morning after I'd wandered, my mother would yell that I couldn't be properly cared for if I kept on buggering off and if I kept on hiding myself when I was home. Then she would crash about at the stove until her husband stopped her and sat her down and looked over at me with the damp brown eyes of some gentle creature, a soft grazing animal no one should force into a combat, or ask to survive after war. And here he was trying to cope with a hair-trigger wife and a son he'd gathered with her on a Tuesday afternoon and brought back from Hampstead like something sent to be washed. Washed or mended. She'd yell about that, too, on occasion.

Like a bundle, you were. All wrapped up in horrible knitting and skinny little knees and elbows. Not enough fat on you, nothing there ready to back you up. They should have seen to that. We sorted you out, though, and you seemed like you were happy to see us. We'd met the once before and you looked at us as if we were familiar. Such a gaze you had, very firm. They said you were two or so. Diddy and tiny chap for your age. You were never a single minute's trouble to us back then.

She'd go on. Dad and me knew that she'd stopped being angry, when she started remembering. And then we'd be quiet together and then we would hug and then we would eat more breakfast than we ought with the rationing still on and even less bacon allowance in peacetime, because we were left by ourselves with none of the Allied countries here to help us any more. My mother was loud and brimstone and then afterwards food and love. Dad and I both liked that about her.

Mum would ask me if I wasn't settled, or I didn't like her and Dad. I'd cry then. I'd cry and hold her. You can't tell anyone, can you, the whole of how you love them? Everything that's true disappears if you try. Mum would ask me if I'd recollected something from the times before we met. There wasn't a trace, though, of other hands and other faces, other countries. I had a sense that I'd been very cold at one time and there were certain scents that scared me, that still do, but that was all. I had no idea of how I'd lived without them. I knew they were mine and I was theirs, that we were each other's people. I didn't go into the past much beyond that, not for a while.

And how can your parents defend you against what you can't recall?

When I'd look in the mirror later, older, preparing myself to go out and charm girls of an evening – I'd somehow know I wasn't right. I was like the bombsite houses, I had a shake. I'd stand and stare back at my own blue eyes and my hair turned white by the summer sun, or yellow as butter in winter, and I'd change my plans. I'd stay at home, play cribbage with my dad and listen to the wireless, do normal things like a normal person, like my mother's son, my father's son. Of course, I'm not.

All I knew then was I came to London from an orphanage in Marseille. But that didn't make sense, did it? Why wouldn't they have kept me there in France? Why did I end up in Hampstead in the, my mum said, very dusty tall house of a Catholic old lady who was lapsed, but the nuns weren't to know? The older I got, the more I wondered. But mainly I kept on being a kid. I played games, I went to school, went even if I was sleepy after night-walking. I remember on Sundays I'd have to hunt for the slightly black-market malt tablets that Dad hid for me around the furniture – the same number of tablets as the years in my age. (My guessed age on my July invented birthday.) We'd do that when we needed cheering and I don't remember when we stopped. Maybe I got into double figures and that was too many tablets, or we'd run out, or I'd lost interest in wanting them, or searching. I seem selfish to myself when I look back at that. Dad seemed to enjoy it as much as me and I took it from him.

Then sweets were off the ration – everything was – you could get them fairly easy, but girls tasted better. No disrespect. Just kisses. The flavour of some wonderful other mouth that invites you in is miraculous. You can taste that in your veins. First time a woman opened up her lips and let me in, joined me in a kiss, I thought I'd done it wrong, because I felt weird all of a sudden and so I stopped. The girl, woman, female person, she laughed at me, but in a kind way, and said it was okay.

I told Mum when I got back home – she laughed at me as well. *Of course you felt odd, you're bloody well supposed to, and no you don't have to get married, you bloody lunatic. You're just ...*

She never told me what I was just. I should have asked. From her face, she wasn't thinking of anything bad.

Bloody this, *bloody* that. She used to swear a lot. She even said *fuck*, but only under serious provocation: general elections and the Grand National when her horse went down, which it always did. And in my kid Sundays she'd swear at me and my dad for making her chairs and cushions and everywhere smell malty – *Like a sodding bandage.*

The threat of medicines and doctors, anything medical, made her imagine unpleasant scents. And scents – even malty, sweet ones – out of their proper place, somehow became medical in her head. She'd tell me the same thing, over and over – *If you go into a fucking hospital, you never come back out, not alive. That's that.* Which probably was quite accurate in a bit of her lifetime, but things got better after. There was a space when anyone had a fair chance to be well. People had turned optimistic after all the killing and the dying and I think it made them understand how wickedness worked and do the opposite. They hadn't liked the end results from cruelty and so they made things better for each other. It wasn't them being nice, it was about surviving. Optimism doesn't last, though, because the effort takes it out of you too much. Being optimistic means you're always resisting the world.

Going into a hospital now, I wouldn't like it. You don't want to think you won't leave again, do you? We're back to that way of being frightened and it's a shame.

She complained at the end, Mum did, about how the bloody hospital smelled of bloody malt, which it didn't.

The ward was parade-ground shiny, then. Nice nurses – she made them laugh. I'm not sure now if she was maybe joking about the malt, or else trying to make her corner of a four-bed bay in Woolcott Ward fade away and let her be in her old sitting room, back in the years when we were all together and Dead was never going to find us.

I can't ask her about it now, can I?

It makes sense that she wanted to slide off into one of our Sundays, because our Sundays were the best. We made a point of never going near a church – unlike some of the neighbours – and we would be righteous at home instead, because we were Socialists, which was going to be the future. We were going to be Paradise on Earth. And God wouldn't be able to bother anybody and no one would end up beguiled by Capital's demons.

When I married Julie, though, we did it in a church. We were an anti-establishment couple, but we fancied some stained glass, as well. We didn't think that God would mind us. The summer of 1971 and she's in cheesecloth and I'm in these faded jeans and a mess of a shirt. Wild flowers in armfuls. We wanted to bring back love to the building, or something, there was definitely a theory. That and so many colours and so many kisses and this silly sod with a guitar.

I remember the afternoon shining, it sneaked through the weave of her dress and there she was and we were going to belong to each other. And this poor, affronted vicar was doing his best and staying polite and you and everyone could feel all these intellectual contradictions, fizzing against your skin, until Steve, he was my best friend, read out how love is patient and love is kind and all those other things and that fizzed, too, that ached down the length of me.

That bloody guitarist. I thought he was Julie's fault and she thought he was mine. I have no idea where he came from to this day. He got irritating, but then Steve spoke out that long, sweet ribbon of words that were nothing but centuries of love and we agreed with it entirely – Julie and me. We assumed we were going to have angels' tongues and power over mountains, because why not?

All of the guys looked like Jesus and all of the girls there were aiming to be Mary. I can't say which Mary. We were in Galilee on Thames.

By then I'd found out that I came to Marseille from a place called Artlenburg in Lower Saxony. I'd written to the nuns in anxious French and found out that an officer in the Fife and Forfar Yeomanry had sent me like a black-market parcel out of Germany and into France. I wanted to ask him why: if it was to make up for the bombing, our bombing that answered their bombing, that turned into ruins everywhere. You might want to take a baby out of that.

So I stood at the altar thinking I was German, but English now. I was two countries together and that was maybe a good idea, a peaceful idea. We believed in peace then. And sat behind me in a pew were her parents and Mum and Dad. They were dressed for another decade, but that was all right. It's only that I had this feeling for a tiny while as if I would never hold on to them again, not touch them. It scared me. I suppose it's normal to be afraid at your own wedding, isn't it?

I noticed there was a moment when Mum stopped pretending to be happy for me. She thought I'd gone wrong and hadn't told me, because you don't, do you? With adults that you care for, you have to restrain your advice.

Mum did have a habit of laughing at marriages – *She thinks he's smiling, cos he's got a wondrous secret. He's just scared silly – look at him, his balls have gone into hiding.* She made Dad grin – *Thank fuck they're only ruining each other, they serve themselves right* – and then she'd touch his hand, or his shoulder, or kiss his ear. They'd have a bit of a cuddle. She was a very unselfish woman, but somewhere in her was this competition with every other husband and especially every wife. She knew she was winning.

After Dad went she lost that as well.

When I started out with Julie, I'd want us to seem contented in the world, to win. It annoyed her. We were not contented and she didn't like having to act. She wanted reality and I wanted something softer. And I kept on being not quite there and she kept on telling me about it. She had the same things to complain about as Mum, except the flat we first moved into had no shaking, so I didn't go out in the nights. I'd dream of running sometimes in the dawn and the streets keeping me in their arms and I should have been looking for that with my wife. But we make mistakes, don't we?

No kids.

We started to feel temporary and nobody ought to bring children into that. Julie went to work and so did I and sometimes we seemed happy and I started to search for that captain in the Fife and Forfars. I made my research a way to fill our evenings.

Captain McNeill was killed stepping on a landmine six months after Jodl signed the surrender. His staff sergeant, though – a man called Collins – eventually I found him. At first he was nervous, sitting in the snug of this pub that was his local. He'd settled in Guildford, so not far. I got the train one Sunday, didn't tell Julie. I should have.

The man looked at his beer and then looked at another. His third pint let him meet my eyes, my blue eyes. In the end he told me who I am.

McNeill was given this baby by a woman in Berlin, British sector. She'd been married to a Nazi, lost or taken at Stalingrad – either way, Dead would have got him. In the happy days of nothing but fighting success her husband had brought a baby home from Poland, Radom, she thought. He could do what he liked, so he did that, took another couple's baby because it looked Aryan and they were Slavic so they couldn't keep it. Those were hands that touched me, carried me, covered in the sweat you get with madness. Aryan race, Aryan bollocks, but he picked me up like a seashell from a beach – *here's a point of interest in amongst this trash, these people who are trash*. Everything else got drowned with the turn of the tide.

I was late back after that and had another row. And all through it I kept thinking – what would they have turned me into if they'd won? And was I a terrible husband because of that sweat, that hate sweat, touching me?

Staff Sergeant Collins said the Berlin woman didn't want me in the house, not any longer, because I marked her with her husband's guilt, because she'd hated the man her father made her marry, because she couldn't love the kids he'd made her bear. She wanted me to escape her and never know.

You do have to know, though, don't you? And I could think of her maybe hating a kid because of how it looked, the blond and blue. I could understand that.

I'm the only man I know who was happy when his hair turned grey. It felt like breaking free.

The row after Guildford, I thought it would finish us. I thought I knew why I wouldn't get close to Julie, couldn't, why Mum would shake her head at me when she'd got me by myself in the kitchen. I thought I'd always known I was infectious.

What made us all right was a Lazarus house.

We'd moved out to a place in Greenwich, which neither of us really liked, but it was as close to a compromise as we could get, being who we were just then. We had money, but no joy in it. Our third or fourth week with boxes still left to unpack, I woke up and the air was shaking. And I understood.

Bombsite.

But you can't leave all of a sudden in the middle of the night when you're trying to be a married man, it's not acceptable. So I came down quiet and sat at the kitchen table while these little ghosts of purgatory banged about. I made a cup of tea and held it and maybe I was making this *shhhhh, shhhhh* noise through my teeth. Julie always told the story of this night to people later – winning her own kind of competition – and I reckon she added the *shhhhh* bit in. Then again, it might have been true, I might have been trying to comfort the house.

I looked up from the table and saw her. She was wearing this big nightgown, to keep away from me in our bed. I did the same with pyjamas. I was sitting there, cold in these stupid pyjamas, old-man pyjamas, and running through my head what I could possibly try to say.

I could have talked about love until it disappeared. That wouldn't have fixed us, would it? But the new house had already saved us. The shaking had woken her, too. Anyone could have seen that in her face, although it took me a while, because I'm stupid, aren't I? Sometimes I'm dim.

And what I said to her then was – *It's all right now, though. We've got through. Peaceful.* It was as if I'd been practising every sleepless time for that one very early morning when I'd be woken and be with her and be allowed to fall in love. Those two different frightened houses had taught me what to do and they didn't have to. They owed me nothing. They weren't speaking to the war in me, to any badness, they were just crying because sometimes everything has to.

We sat side by side at the kitchen table and we cried. And afterwards everything was just the same, but completely different. Easy. We got easy. It didn't take long before we were no trouble, before we were slightly Paradise. And the house shook, now and again, and we didn't mind, because it took away the fear in us, bit by bit. That's how it seemed. The pair of us, leaning at the table, shoulders touching and *shhhhh* and this process had started and it made us laugh.

Next time we visited Mum, she noticed the change in us as soon as we walked in. She hugged me. Tight. Like bloody fury.

In the hospital on her last afternoon she hugged me again and she got me to lean in and listen and she told me – *I never thought you'd manage, but you did. You put the work in, you and her. You always were a battler.*

Dad went first, like a gentleman. After his funeral – dressed for a decade when they were young – Mum walked back to the big black car we'd hired, holding my arm. She seemed to be making her way through a stream that had never been there before and anxious in case it stole her feet from under her. She said – *What am I going to do now, then? What the hell am I going to do now?*

Without him she was still herself, still had a laugh, still swore, but every pavement seemed to frighten her a bit. Her steps got shorter.

That's how I walk now – my mother's way. I'm not secure. And when the house wakes me and I want to get out and feel the dark making me welcome, it doesn't work. I get too tired and the house is impatient and it wants to talk to Julie, as well as me, and it can't, can it?

I should have gone first, like a gentleman. I intended to, I swear. Not that I hoped to leave Julie, not that I didn't want God to make her Paradise, but we all do get taken away. Dead's always waiting and I thought, perhaps I thought, that the place up ahead could seem more pleasant if I was already there. I could stay close and be waiting like. Then we'd be Socialists in Paradise and that would make us laugh.

Some idea like that.

Religion is the opium of the masses, but sometimes you need anaesthetic and opium would be good. I can think that, can't I?

Of course, I don't believe in Paradise and we didn't build one here. Everyone stopped trying. I wish we'd done better. Battle on for Paradise and you won't get there, but wherever you are, it'll be good. Dad used to say that and Mum would agree.

I used to feel sorry for people who died in a cruel time and didn't get to see the change, the February '45 people, June '45 – the ones who nearly made it to their ceasefire. I can't talk about that to people, can I? I can't tell them I won't last long enough to see the next change. I can't talk about bombsite houses, I've never met anyone else who understands them. I can't ask them questions, because they can't answer, the strangers out there.

I can't say to anyone – *What am I going to do now, then? What the hell am I going to do now?*

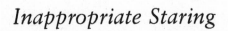

Inappropriate Staring

B elieve it or not, I came here for the choughs: *Pyrrhocorax pyrrhocorax*. If you don't know, they're a black bird with red feet and beaks, athletic build – if you can say that of a bird – and they sound pretty much like somebody in a cave playing the kazoo. Yes, that would be their call – the sound of a troglodyte who had managed to find a kazoo. They flaunt their athleticism at cliff faces, are not especially endangered any more, but are of conservation concern.

This incident takes place a few years ago and – long story – although I have often been offered the chance to see choughs, something has always happened thus far to prevent me. I have seen them since, but at the time of telling, I have not. Otherwise sturdy cars have broken down on chough-seeing excursions, weather and light have failed on my arrival in guaranteed chough territory and so forth. And, by this point – long story – I am in Jersey for a funeral, or rather for its aftermath, and I have realised: *Jersey Zoo has captive choughs*. I decide I will leave off clearing a house and going through papers and telling utility companies their last bill has been paid, winding up the symptoms of a life, and I will make a day trip out to Trinity and I will see choughs. Finally.

This is the Durrell zoo I'm talking about, the one I always wanted to visit when I was a kid and yet never reached. My life at home contained many, largely frustrated, ambitions. But I wanted to read Gerald Durrell – Uncle Mort told me about him – and I did manage that. I ate up all his books, but his tales of a Corfu childhood in shorts and sunshine and imbued with wonderful freedoms were the narratives that stuck. I adopted his experiences as my right. To the untrained observer, I might have been nervous and over-regulated, but inside I was desperate to be reckless. I was not surrounded by benign adults and fascinating languages and even more fascinating creatures, but I felt that I could be at some point, I aimed for it.

We did have a cat.

It ran away. I choose to suspect it found us boring.

I couldn't follow the cat of course – I was too young – but somewhere, perhaps when I slept, wild curiosity and improvisation in the presence of beauty belonged to me. It felt proper that animals ought to be cared for (I missed the cat) and that human beings should also be preserved in their natural states of eccentricity and salt-watery warmth and enjoyable national differences.

And there was always Uncle Mort. He was benignly warm, enjoyable and different, but far away and apparently unable to visit me. In lieu of more personal expositions, he sent me books listing birds I could watch for, flowers, trees and – this volume was immediately forbidden – the varied forms of native fungi, both tasty and fatal.

I knew I couldn't insist on seeing Uncle Mort, or make my liking for him over-evident. He wasn't family and you were supposed to love your family the most. 'Uncle Mort' was simply a form of address invented, I believe, by my mother. Family or not, he was always a little door into the sunshine. Poor Not Uncle Mort.

'Look at that one.'

'Where?'

'The little one. There. He's a cheeky one, isn't he?'

On the day in question, by the time I climb onto the tourist bus that winds through clotted-cream countryside and hamlets towards the zoo, I am relatively excited. I am about to fulfil two small ambitions while – long story – being on Jersey and doing sad things.

'Where?'

'There. Right there. You don't know how to spot them, you don't.'

Once I'm at the zoo it's nice. It has many nice aspects: kiddies running squealingly and freely and informatively labelled plants and trees and loose herds of mildly unusual ducks. The lemurs are nice, the enclosures are nice – there's nothing wrong with the place. The clever-eyed tamarins – nice.

I know Durrell is long dead. Intellectually, I am aware of this, but still it sideswipes me to pass the tree his survivors planted in his memory and to read the little plaque beneath which indicates Gerald Malcolm Durrell's remains are in that area.

His absence must be sad for him and those who loved him. But standing at the tree and reading the plaque – which is mainly about the irreplaceability of species – I also felt intimately, personally sad. I might have just learned I had lost a family member. Of course, I had only lost a vestigial part of myself. Durrell was supposed to be alive forever, like Prince Caspian, or Paddington Bear. He is meant, even now, to be swimming somewhere in a phosphorescent evening ocean, or clapping his sandals down a dusty track.

In the shade of that tree, I realise a deep idea of mine has always been that I will eventually grow up while being lost under sun and happy and eating warm fruit as I pick it. I have believed there would still be time for me to arrange this.

That I have already grown up, under quite different circumstances, insists on being very obvious and sudden – like a facial injury. Something is finished forever, has been for decades. No chances to go tomboying about in middle age. Undignified. And I am not a wealthy woman. Even living somewhere hot and economically blighted, I would barely have savings to last a year.

'Where?'

'There. Right there. You don't know how to spot them, you don't.'

I grew up to be responsible, mildly in profit most years, never actually underwater and highly self-regulated. I am not quite as dull as my father. I am not quite as anxious as my mother. My son Peter, an only child, is discernibly an improvement that Nature has made upon me. I trust that evolution could continue to perfect my descendants until they become reliably happy. But I also anticipate that economic and political pressures, along with ecological disasters, will probably defeat them. I have emphasised happiness when perhaps the slow development of ingenuity and endurance would have been more use. It's all out of my hands.

I find I am remembering Peter's father – as it happens, also a bearded alcoholic – as I read Durrell's plaque. I wonder if I will ever see him again – my ex-partner, not dead Durrell. Then I drift into the couple of rooms set aside and filled with Durrell artefacts – the sort of stuff people find in your house once you're dead: not quite useful, but sentimentally tenacious. Unless you have a great deal of storage space and one eye on a possible archive, it's just clutter that a regular spring cleaning should prevent.

They call it death cleaning these days and blame it on Sweden. Everything now is about death, apparently. I refuse, not that anyone's asking, to exist for the convenience of those who will outlive me. They get to keep on being alive and I feel that's a big plus for them already, I don't owe them further favours. And if they liked me they'll be sad no matter what – that's how bereavement works. I'm not going to try and micro-manage how bad they're going to feel, or how they choose to mourn, or to forget me. They will be alive, they will be none of my business. My son will be none of my business. Tidying me up will give everyone something to do. If they care, they will need something to do in those first days: I'll give them that. I'm not going to sleep in a coffin eating ready meals I buy one at a time, waiting in an empty flat hard by a graveyard just to spare them inconvenience.

Peter will manage. He will become less solitary. He will find someone. He will stop being like me.

He can give my things away to people – people always need things, they're useful.

'Where?'

'There. Right there. You don't know how to spot them, you don't.'

All of which I mention to establish that the whole of my zoo outing has turned depressing by this stage and – long story – Jersey is a bit of a downer, too. And I'm slightly lost – thirty-two acres are available, after all – but I eventually do find the bird area and, within it, the location of the aviary for the choughs.

Naturally, quite naturally, there are no choughs.

They are not that remarkable, choughs, you needn't go climbing trees in the Hesperides to find one, they're not like some of the other creatures here – practically unicorns, manticores, baby krakens – they're just choughs. But I did come all this way and I do need cheering and they're not here to cheer me. And they're mixed up with my childhood and wearing sandals and liking fun and encountering – that's the verb I want – encountering miraculous livingness.

I needed that.

The day in question is one when I really need some choughs.

The choughs have been moved, allegedly, not to baffle me, but because their accommodation is being upgraded: water slides and trampolines, massage tables, I don't know. Maybe choughs are demanding. Maybe the zoo authorities will reconstruct their tiny reservation with an eighty-foot cliff inside for aerial playtimes. They would like that.

'Where?'

'There. Right there. You don't know how to spot them, you don't.'

Principal fact to remember – there are no choughs. And I know I ought to trudge about in the midst of all this unmythological and yet still wonderful wonder and enjoy it, but I feel disinclined. I have left – long story – Not Uncle Mort's house behind me and I sort of miss it, while also being pained by its existence. I am thirsty. I have mislaid the way to the restaurant. I am, to be precise, really thirsty. I understand the zoo has to be generously proportioned. They're trying to save all life on earth, or something like that – the kind of enterprise that would take space – but just a vending machine, or else a water fountain every thousand yards or so, would be really helpful.

Very thirsty.

It will be hours until the next bus takes me back to the surly substance abuse and architectural shine of St Helier, its offshore money breeding recklessly out of sight in secure enclosures. Then I'll get a cab back to Not Uncle Mort's. I won't sleep well – long story – surrounded by the boxes of books, wrapped parcels and stacks of paper. He was in the navy, so he left no mess – the masses and masses of paper pulp and ink and information were stowed neatly away. There still are masses and masses, unmanageable masses of stuff, though. They overwhelm me. I can't imagine how his joists withstood the weight.

And this, when I'm not in a glorious mood, is when I come upon the crowd, the thick ring of people surrounding a picturesque and suitably entertaining island. It's where they detain the gorillas, those talismanic, huge, almost-people with reproachful eyes.

'Where?'

'There. Right there. You don't know how to spot them, you don't.'

And also there is this man and this woman, their voices like a swift jab to your ear. Nevertheless, I begin by being glad of them. They're a distraction.

'Oh, yeah ... Fast, isn't he?'

'And cheeky.'

'He's into everything. Look at that.'

'I was looking. You were the one that didn't notice him.'

There are people in life who can only exist by explaining their every experience out loud, as a kind of reassuring chyron, ticking along at the foot of their personal screens. They love sitting on trains and narrating their passing emotional states into phones which may or may not be connected. The habit seems needy but I've never quite known which particular need it speaks to.

Man's voice. 'Is it a him?'

Woman's voice. 'Of course. A girl wouldn't be like that. Girls aren't into everything. Girls are quiet. Should be.'

I love it when women are sexist, it doesn't at all make the whole of my woman's heart stumble, because, goodness knows, we shouldn't stick together. I can already guess how she'd take my singled-handed existence. My being left by Peter's father would be my fault. My losing interest in being betrayed again would be unnatural.

A boy needs his father.

Well, I did try telling his father that.

But she's a person of her generation: grew up seeing mums in the kitchen, women taking care, women saying yes, or saying nothing. People are shaped and can't often resist it. They are even punished if they try. And anyone can love anything, given time – even misery.

The man runs on, almost jovial, but with an edge. 'You can't tell, though, can you? Not with that lot. I mean, they're all like that. See? Running about and climbing and getting in everywhere ... Whole swarm of them.' He laughs down his nose at a not very private joke, considering he's almost shouting.

And this is when I get the wince in my stomach, the tension. It's a much more familiar tension now – as I said, this incident happened a few years ago, at a time when it might have been an outlier and not the norm.

'They can't be a swarm – that's bees.'

And I'm on a kind of break here – long story – not a holiday, but a break and breaks are supposed to be pleasant. And I am trying to avoid my repeating recollections of Not Uncle Mort wearing Not Uncle Mort's jackets, rather than their being only full of coat hangers and air. I am putting the jackets away and this gives me something to do. I am bubble-wrapping crockery I never saw him use, because someone will surely want it – we live in a time of unfulfilled and arbitrarily inflicted wants. I am opening – long story – letters and letters and letters, old letters. I am not depressed, but I feel assaulted and much smaller than would be usual when compared to the average size of reality. And I am genuinely disappointed by the lack of bloody choughs and this makes me feel petty. I hate to be petty. And I am thirsty, thirstier every time I swallow. In short, there are numerous reasons for my allowing myself to say something like – *Oh, and now I have to listen to racism as well*. But instead I keep my head down. I act like a coward here. I am a coward – if I'm acting like one, then I am one. I don't say a word. I pretend that I have probably misheard the little whistle for the nasty dog and fight hard to assume that I am, in fact, mistaken and no harm has been meant.

The man of the pair does not help me with this. 'He'd be in your windows and up on the roof and sitting on your chairs all at once ... That's a fact. I've read they're very strong. Impulsive – that's the word.'

The woman has the 1950s accent she's kept carefully all this time, fastidious about consonants and with aspirational vowels. 'He's a boy. Boys are like that. Look at his little face. That's a boy, that is. And there's his little fingers.'

The man has a voice invented not so long ago, apparently with the sole intention of more perfectly expressing angry whiteness. 'There's his dirty little fingers.' His underlying fury may be further stoked by the fact that his choice makes him sound, now and then, exactly like an urban black kid of the 1990s. He must occasionally make himself want to cut out his own tongue and that's surely unpleasant.

Then again, speaking as a white person, I am very tired of angry whiteness.

And I am very thirsty. And my childhood was not my childhood, it belonged to Gerald Durrell and he is dead in the way that Not Uncle Mort is also dead and Mort was the only person who ever let me scamper along cliffs in sunshine and I saw him maybe once a year – came out and stayed with him in Jersey maybe once a year – until the time when everything stopped and I didn't know why. It's as if I got orphaned early.

And there are no fucking choughs.

And now here is this. This. This couple talking, skirting around a definite longing to hate someone out loud.

The woman, a pensioner woman, is in a sun hat and a frilly silly blouse that makes you feel – well, I'm not that sure what: perhaps indulgent towards her. And you are also aware that she will need serious health care soon and will find there isn't any. She will be the sort of tiny tragedy that no one much bothers about. She's wearing those slightly medical shoes that are good for swollen feet, a skirt with a flamboyantly cut hem and girlish earrings, which suggest she has fantasy gypsy aspirations, not at all reliant on liking actual gypsies, Roma, Sinti, in any way.

So I'm maybe not the only one with unsuitable ideas about how I'll eventually turn out when I'm a grown-up, really a grown-up, not just older and more dog-eared, actually a grown-up.

She's sporting a very fresh perm. She's having a day out, is what that perm says. She's a person, a human person with just enough money, but you can see things are tight. Everything about her is both inexpensive and not hard-wearing. Still, she's brought it all together with consideration. She wants to look nice. People want to look nice.

The man beside her has the same flatliner mouth and the same pendulous earlobes. He is a little more overweight than she is, but it's a close-run thing: cargo shorts, check shirt with the sleeves rolled. The cloth is tense across his back and grips his biceps with a kind of desperation. Sandals with Velcro straps. I can't see him that well, can't see his face at all, because his mother is nearer to me and conceals him. I'm assuming she's his mother. Human people have relatives, they care for them and take them – gawdhelpus – go with them – gawdhelpus – to the zoo.

The mother, let's call her a mother, is beginning to look anxious. You can guess that she has experience of his going off on one, having read the paper of a morning and such-like. She offers, 'Well, he's been playing, hasn't he? Oh, and here's mum ... ' And at this point a female gorilla does amble in with some urgency towards what may indeed be her infant. 'She's not happy with him, you can tell. I can tell ... A mother knows a mother, no matter what. You can be different as anything, but a mother knows when she sees a mother. And he's caught on that she's cross – he's nervous. Wants to hold her hand. You always wanted to hold my hand when I was going to give you a row, remember? She'll clout him, I bet.' She is creating patter as a distraction.

So I'm fairly sure now that the woman is his mum, the man's mum. And she is also as splendid a passive-aggressive heap of voluntary weakness as you can probably find in the assembled gorilla-viewing multitude.

While thinking this I also – I have to – reproach myself for being judgemental and acknowledge that she does, after all, have this angry son and may have an angry husband and more large, angry sons at home. She may have very few options when it comes to strategy and self-defence.

People do have strategies. Their efforts may be ineffective, but they make them, just the same. We all tend to try what we can.

'Well, she can't give him a row, can she? They don't exactly speak.' Her son is very good at contempt. It appears to be his strategy and self-defence. And he is perhaps feeling uneasy because he is perhaps the kind of son with no idea of how to entertain his mother, who simply takes her for the kind of treats a kid would like, maybe the kind of treats she once gave him.

History does repeat itself. I am more like my mother than I knew.

Both she and my father are dead and cleared away, so I have no opportunity to confer, but I believe close examination of my fine detail would reveal more and more of her.

'They understand each other.'

'I doubt it ... Ah – you didn't expect that. Wrong there, weren't you?' The mother gorilla scoops up her round-eyed offspring and pets her, or him – it's not rude to check when you're looking at animals – and she is indulgent, dextrous, fastidious.

'Giving him cuddles instead. Well, that's sweet. He's got round her. That's how you used to get round me – give me the big brown eyes and put up your arms for a hug.' Oh, Mother, you are a one.

The man leans forward and I can see the flash of reddish energy in the eyes, the face which is pre-furious, in the habit of rage. The skin is tinted with frustration and an irritating life. He is a person and must be in a kind of constant, human pain to look that way. This is sad, if not a full-blown tragedy, playing out for random and possibly selected audiences. If we don't care, he may wish to make us.

Because I am now frankly staring their way, his glance dunts against mine and gets quizzical and then intentionally bleak.

He dips down to the woman and delivers, 'Dunno what you mean ... ' as if he is in a British noir movie of my youth, or thereabouts. You could guess he doesn't practise in his mirrors, because he is constantly practising in life:

the postures of an aggrieved, hard-done-by man. If he finds a good reason to let loose and fully flower – if he gets drunk enough, stoned enough, outraged enough – then he will be a trouble. He will be the kind of self-harm that hurts other people first.

The possibility of this hair-trigger man still living in his mother's house is concerning and raises a sweat on my hands while he again glances my way. It becomes a point of honour that I don't break eye contact. I am a single-handed woman, we can do that kind of thing. We often have to.

He moves from an expression of growing outrage to the kind of pop-eyed, pouting mask you offer to someone you think is unbalanced – that is, if you enjoy mocking the mentally unstable.

So to him I am just another crazy female. There aren't so many ways for female people to behave in his world and I've crossed one of his lines. This is his way of ignoring me: I am a funny mad object, not a dignified and sobering moral judgement. This is a shame because I was sort of hoping to be meaningful. If I ask him now why he is being racist he will repeat his little pout and maybe roll his eyes and tell me he's just talking about monkeys. This is a guess, but it's not a guess based on a lack of experience. There are so many ways, in our time, to talk about things without having to admit it. Our ambient hatreds are both violent and spineless.

But I'm also assuming here that he doesn't know gorillas are apes, rather than monkeys, and that's unfair of me.

Then again, I know for sure that he doesn't know people are people. All people are people always – even the broken ones like him – but he's trying to dodge it. This is a problem for everyone, but also vexes him. Presumably, in a personal taxonomy where species status slips so easily, he must have to work very hard and then even harder to justify his own position. He mustn't like the wrong music, must never enjoy the wrong food, mustn't smile out at streets as he walks in case he blesses the wrong face with his approval and gets tainted. He must work so hard to avoid factual information: history, geography, biology, anthropology, love.

I did love Not Uncle Mort, I discover. I did that consistently. I am not clearing that away.

It seems that he also loved me back. In Not Uncle Mort's house there were boxes full of appropriate love for a child who is not your possession: affection and advice held in storage. There were hundreds of letters, perhaps over a thousand letters I never received that would have made my younger self delighted, inclined to be different in a better future.

What I'm saying is that, as this all unfurls, not one of us seems to be really at our best. People are not always at their best.

The mother, meanwhile, and I begin to like her for it, is sticking in her sharp, maternal knife. 'You still do that with me. Early training, that is. You get spoiled. Do you carry on like that with Pauline?' She's says *Pauline* the way someone else might say *Herpes*.

'Why would Pauline want to give me a row?' His head snaps towards her – and me – again. His colour flushes a deeper shade of beerandsunbed.

It is my turn to present the face of someone who finds what they see less than impressive. I'm not sure if there is a facial expression that accurately conveys *Oh, so your girlfriend is a useless tart* ... ? But I am trying for it.

This is childish of me, but – no choughs.

He twitches his lips back from his teeth.

His mother pursues her point. 'I should imagine she'd have lots of reasons. Why isn't she here, anyway?' I briefly wonder if her husband is long dead from having had his points pursued, run to ground like foxes and torn apart.

Other people's domestic arrangements are often surprising. Mort's chosen lifestyle was crowded with ink and wood pulp. His spare room was lined with bookcases. He called it *my library*. If he didn't know about something, he would make sure he found out. This was a habit he passed on. Inheritance becomes easy when it's accompanied by love – you run towards it then. Most of all when I was sent to stay with him – lone little-girl passenger being spoiled by staff on the ferry over – Not Uncle Mort just let me play. He let me run down from Le Mont des Vignes to the beach. Sometimes he went with me – a salt-watery, sun-faded adult who held my hand – and then he'd tell me what everything was called. I wasn't interested in minerals or cloud shapes, but I loved naming animals. I would christen them first and those names would be used for them day-to-day.

Dry Armed Lizard Bird, Blood Gull, Shouting Tail.

The proper Latin appellations Mort would keep with him and dole out at intervals: *Phalacrocorax carbo, Larus argentatus, Sylvia undata.*

Cormorant, Herring Gull, Dartford Warbler – there are so many ways to say the same thing, depending on who you are. The naming is always about you, not about what you're naming.

I was never very sure why my parents sent me for so many summers, to stay with a man who seemed to be almost a stranger to them. I simply accepted those young Jersey summers of peace while my parents undoubtedly yelled at each other in my absence, just as they did when I was there. I never considered the shape of mouth and shape of ears I shared with Not Uncle Mort. I never did notice when I was practising in my mirrors, that I wasn't just trying out being myself, but also being him. Or I thought it was only love and not genetics, too.

And meanwhile the man explains his girlfriend's, or wife's, or whatever's absence with 'Work. She's working.' This is a bit of a mumble and may signal a defeat. Perhaps Pauline is, as suspected, a terrible person. Or perhaps being married to, or in a relationship with, him produces strange behaviour.

They are all people, though, all human beings: the man, the mother, invisible, terrible Pauline. Every one of them is human.

'Didn't want to be with the mother-in-law.' The woman is the man's mother, then. 'Avoiding me.' She manages to sound, if not like a stiletto, then like a knitting needle being brandished and now they're fully fighting and I can relax. They are only hating each other – and one absent human being – they are not being sweeping. They sound like all my Christmas holidays when I was kid – familiar. My shoulders drop and I realise how high they have been cranked.

Sniping, growling, slander, threats: that's the noise of any household, isn't it, any home? Peter and I didn't fight, not at all, but I chose to feel we were unusual. I decided that if I'd let some other someone in, sat him down on the living-room sofa, led him upstairs, then battles would inevitably start. I only ever had true faith in the solidity of peace when I was with Mort.

The man over-enunciates, no doubt hotly, into his mother's face, as if he's explaining particle physics to a cretin, 'She's working. I said.' Then he softens, pondering. 'They must be strong ... Her lifting him like that. I mean, he's got to be a bit of a weight.' The man peers at the island and its gorillas and gorilla toys, gorilla-worthy enrichment and stimulation – the friendliest possible type of imprisonment.

Mother ponders with him, eager to fall in step. 'She'll be used to it. And they are strong, aren't they? I mean, they're stronger than us.'

'They're all stronger than us – all of them – that's the problem.' I can almost feel his testicles wince from here. 'Used to pick them for the heavy labour, didn't they? Better than horses.' His voice peaks a little on this, but then he drops his arm down fondly onto his mother's shoulders. 'Stronger than you, old doll.'

'Cheeky boy.' She smiles, glances about, shows us all the face of somebody in love with her child. People love their children, would die and suffer for them without hesitation, struggle and climb and swim. She ticks her head slightly against his chest. He's a full eighteen inches taller than her and this is easily arranged.

The gorillas potter, eat, groom. The young ones scramble about deftly with adventurous ease and strength, much as I intended I would in my alternative existence.

The son targets his mum with the kind of crooningly expressed criticism I imagine is familiar to every toxic living room across the nation and beyond. 'Sitting about and staring at the telly, eating chocolate Brazils and mini pizzas ... why would you be strong ... ? Pauline does spinning and free weights and all that – *cardiovascular.*'

Mother removes her head and her approval. The truce is over. 'Personal trainer now, are you? And I don't want to look like a weightlifter. She'll end up built like a bloke. She's got mannish shoulders.'

'She's got stamina.' He puts a blare of sex in his delivery and glances over at me again.

'Don't be disgusting to your mother. And what would you want me to have stamina for – cleaning the kitchen?'

'When do you clean that kitchen?'

'Cheeky boy ... I spoiled you.'

'Yeah, I'm horrible ... I'm a terrible son.' He pauses and then – 'Hey, do you think that one's ill? Him under the blanket.' He focuses on me again. 'I wonder where they get the blankets ... I bet people send them. Morons'll send in anything anyone asks for. Soft.'

I don't think gorillas do actually ask for anything. I think we owe them, but I don't think they necessarily ask. I wish they could. I wish everything could – the din of that, how could we stand it?

Before I got out to the zoo, I should mention I spent all morning – all night and then the early morning – reading letters returned to sender which had been for me. I never got them. I never got the Christmas presents, either – still wrapped and boxed up and in stacks. Sometimes my home address is scored through and Mort's is written out firmly in my father's hand, sometimes it's my mother's. Joint effort, then.

I am still processing this.

And there are no choughs.

The man keeps aiming over his mother's head and at me. 'In past the fences, quick as you like, and then they need blankets and food and money and we always just give 'em everything we've got.'

Mother is bewildered by this, but skims across it in a way that suggests she's had practice. 'What, him? Leastways, I think it's a him.' I picture her watching silently while her husband rants, being a nice quiet woman in various sitting rooms, the one whose opinions you never get to know. 'Can't get much of an idea about him, can we . . . ? No, he's sleeping, I think. And I suppose they feel the cold the way we do. Or a bit, anyway.'

They are now permanently talking about two things at once. I am hearing this mildly nasty and yet playful conversation and also this simultaneous series of horrible somethings. My forehead feels prised-apart and baffled and this sensation is unfamiliar to me at that time.

I could have written to Mort. I did miss him. When you're young, though, and have examinations and worries and boyfriends – things fall away. And I was hurt – I thought that he had abandoned me, so I abandoned him back.

But he'd bought a present for each of my Christmases and each birthday – slowly changing with my age and guessed-at expansion of interests. They dated from my first summer without him and were prescient, kept on being prescient, kept on filling unfillable gaps of need, waking them and filling them and causing this type of metaphorical blood loss. The last returned parcel must have come home to him after my parents moved house.

It has the angry addition of GONE AWAY! in some stranger's thick-inked printing. After that he'd still bought things, still packed them up, even though he had nowhere to send them.

In public conversations my dad always called him *a friend of your mother's* when I dragged any conversation round to him. Mum called him nothing at all. And then usually there was a row when they got back indoors and were left to their own devices.

'Could be hiding – I've seen 'em do that. There are videos online. I showed you. Maybe he's hiding. They get in everywhere, like cockroaches.'

I don't watch the TV news any more because it gives me that prised-apart feeling. I avoid quite a lot of TV, in fact. Stick to nature programmes.

'No. They're too big to be cockroaches, silly. And we can see him.'

'It's not us he's hiding from, is it? Otherwise this wouldn't be a zoo.'

'I've read they creep about. Or someone told me. Soft on their feet.'

News creeper – that's what they call the chyron, there to creep at the bottom of your news. It's all creeping, isn't it? We live in a time of creeping.

The important news – all humans are human – is the news you never get. Your mother maybe had an affair with this man and maybe there was a great deal of complication and certainly he loved you – that's important news. Mort told his solicitor that he loved me and wanted that to be recorded when they made out his will – important news. And who can say how I would properly name Mort at this point, but I want to very much – important news. The important news is the news you never get.

I want to tell him things. I still want to tell him things.

And in dead Durrell's zoo, the son begins really enjoying his paranoia. 'We don't know how they do it, but they all communicate. It stands to reason they've got ways of knowing each other and they'll have fights with some and like others and they'll make their plans …'

'I think people send in blankets and stuff for them to have and do what they want with. I think.' Mother has noticed that I'm not the only one staring and is trying to specifically address the issues of gorillas, even if it means suddenly returning to the blanket issue.

'And they'll fancy each other …'

'Don't say that.'

'Why not? It's just nature. It's just mating. It's animals making other animals, like big snakes make little snakes. That's why you've got to keep the numbers down. You don't let 'em in, or you'll get outbred. You'll get extinct. Want that, do you? Us in a cage and they come and watch us, film us mating.'

I genuinely think this would have made Mort laugh. I am overcome with this memory of him flicking up his hands in pale surrender and giving these woofs and gasps of laughter, specifically at absurdity. The absurdity is also dreadful and that would have made him laugh more – the idea of a human being creating exactly the nightmares that will most perfectly torment him.

I would like to be able to laugh myself, but Mort was a man of his time and I am stuck in mine.

'I've told you, don't be disgusting …' The mother turns to me with that shrugging kind of smile I suppose you offer when someone is being himself, but you've noticed that being himself can be a trouble. And it may be the mentions of sex that are making her tug at her fingers and fluster. She tries nudging away her son's thinking, dogged, practised. 'His mum's fond of him. She's carried him all along and up there.'

'So she's a mum – she's his mum. That's just instincts – that's not feelings.'

She says, very softly and clearly, 'But they're just animals, though.' And she indicates the gorillas and it may be that she is saying that animals are animals, but people are people. It may be.

She smiles at me again and there is a whisper of a nod. Her son may not even have heard her, distracted by his self-inflicted horrors. He may truly – can this be the case? – actually think that he is viewing an enclosure of immigrants, refugees, asylum seekers, just a collection of strangeness that is not from round his way. He seems determined to believe this can be true.

He grinds on, getting louder. 'It's the same with anything. When I was six or seven, you remember that cat had kittens and I picked one of them up – just a kid and I didn't know better – and the mother clawed all across the back of my hand.'

'And she was a good cat the rest of the time.'

He had a cat when he was little, so did I. Something in common.

'Not that day. Animals.' He does not indicate the enclo-sure when he says *Animals*.

'Well, she seems fond of him, doesn't she? His mum. We're not the same – but you can tell. That's all I'm saying.'

The mother's eyes cloud slightly and I feel that she is now the one confused about who are animals and what are people.

Mort would have had books about this. He would have understood. Understanding was like his hobby. I do not resemble my Not Father, I resemble Mort.

'Want her round your house, would you? Feed her. Have her kiddie shitting on your floor?'

By this time almost everyone is looking, or half looking, at the man. His mother brushingly touches his arm, as if she would like to leave now. 'All babies mess themselves ...'

She is interrupted by the swaggerbouncy entrance of a silverback. 'Oh, my goodness – he's big. He's a big one.'

The human audience is smoothly engrossed again by animal life, studying the easy motion of so much size, the solemnity in the huge fingers, the delicacy, thoughtfulness as the monstrously gentle ape nibbles something yellow.

'Where'd he come from?'

Mother is delighted in a nervy way. 'He's got a turn of speed. The size of him ... You see pictures in magazines and places, but you don't understand until you see them for yourself.'

'You'd have a heart attack before he even got to you. Just thinking about it ... I bet he'd break your neck and hardly notice, I bet you he could.'

And, this is when she clutches at my hand. It's a hard, dry grip that surprises us both. 'He looked at me.' And we have this weird instant of being amazed together.

'No, not at you. Don't be daft.'

She breaks the contact. 'Yes, he did.' She turns to her son and there's a kind of purity in her insistence. She wants him to join her, needs it.

'He's just looking at everything, it's not at *you*. It's just … you're one of the things in the way of him searching about. He doesn't understand.'

'He looked at me.'

Her son muscles himself nearer and draws his hand down her arm. He kisses the top of her head. 'You're all right – he can't get you. He can't get anywhere near you.'

I would not have thought he would be the kind of man to kiss the tops of heads.

'Sometimes they get out.' Enjoying the sudden inrush of protection.

'There's electric fences and all sorts of stuff. We're safe here.'

'I don't think so.'

And then his sweetness turns. 'It can't be – he's not a person – he can't look like a person looks at you. You said it about that guy in the shop and it can't be. It cannot be because they are animals. They come and they frighten you, they frighten our people and they shouldn't be allowed to, but now we're going to fucking fix it. We're going to fucking end it. It won't happen any more. None of them.' While he punches this out, parade-ground volume, demonstration volume, Saturday-night volume, his mother's mouth moves with other words that are inaudible. She might almost be praying. Her eyes are lowered. He stands, chin lifted and a tight jaw, inviting contradiction, daring it.

And what do you do in these situations? What does a person do when she is so thirsty and there are no choughs and her father was not her father and this other tender and miraculous man was, but she missed the chance to know it – spent a percentage of her life, in fact, resenting him for having dropped her like a worthless thing? What do you do when you are a human being and you have failed because failure is normal, but also you failed because you were pushed out of shape by other people's mistakes and now there is this stress tight in around you – it's through your arms and it's hot in your chest – and it's encouraging fallibility? What do you do when someone is wrong in a way you think is probably a danger? Or wrong in a way that makes you dirty just because you are beside them and your silence might as well be your agreement, your permission? What do you do? What do you say?

Because there is so much to choose from: jolly British soldiers raping and thieving their way across Spain, because that was more fun than fighting Napoleon, the Black Line marching across Tasmania and killing as it went, or torture in Aden, torture in Ulster, concentration camps in Kenya, imposed famines in India, in Ireland, in Highland Scotland? But why would he care about that? Why would that be of interest?

White, First World people in general? Rape and murder in My Lai, Christian missionaries hunting indigenous people in Paraguay – not hundreds of years ago, only fifty. Evangelicals paying for guns to kill schoolteachers in Mozambique? It gets to be overmuch for one person to express.

Well, I speak, anyway, don't I? The words make this violent blur and take my breath. I can't predict which of the words will be a shout and which will be a mumble and the details are immediately unclear. I'm inside a time I don't remember, won't remember, except in shards.

I know that every time I mention rape the mother flinches and she's an old lady and I don't want to disturb her but I keep on. 'You don't know about this? Don't know about the rest of it? Don't know about anything? How superior can you be when everything you like about yourself is based on lies?' And the mother starts crying – big, human tears. 'And other shades of people do other terrible things. People do terrible things – the point is that most of us are trying not to. We keep on trying not to, so that everybody doesn't end up hurt.'

I am, by this time, waiting for the son to hit me, but he is still being surprised and also – as if by a noble instinct – tucking his arm around his mother's waist and holding her cuddled in close. And I'm mostly not shouting, although my throat hurts. I have started to sound like someone else, but I'm not being especially loud – it's only that a silence has now burrowed out around me and made me get obvious. 'You want everyone wrong to go away? Try it. Try getting them out of their homes. Why would they want to? How do you make them? Make their mums? Make their kids. People try to look after their kids. Or do you think you'll like all of that? Would it make you feel good?' The man's neck flushes, as if I've embarrassed him about a first love. 'How many people do you think you'll be able to murder? You think you'll take to it: blood, bodies, wherever you'll put who's left?'

Now, I think I am shouting. Sweating, certainly, and so thirsty, very thirsty. 'If you don't kill everyone, how do you get away with it? Or you'd just like a civil war?' The mother is pale and this is my fault. He is holding her, as if I am the awful person here, the one saying obscenities. And that's true. 'Peacekeepers coming in later to mop up the blood?' Someone has taken my arm and I don't know who. 'When streets start blowing up what will you do?'

I know that I'm doing this stupidly, badly, and should stop now. 'When you start losing, how will you manage the running away? People don't like refugees.' The touch on my arm insists a little more strongly. 'Don't you know what dead is? Don't you understand it? People never want death, not for anyone they love. And anyone will do anything to keep living and keep safe, so you never let killing, you never let any of this shit out in the open air. Not ever. Because you don't know, you don't know where you'll take us.'

And no one is watching the tranquil and blunt-fingered gorillas any more.

I'm feeling transparent and nauseous. I could believe that everyone around me just at this point can see my veins and fluids and my brain, all the pieces of me being poorly constituted and very soft.

The son is almost purple with suppressing what I'd guess are the things he can't say and can't do in front of his mother and the crowd. Both of them seem unsteady for different reasons and for a moment I could swear that our racing breaths keep time, keep time, keep time.

The mother's weeping has diminished into sobs, quieter, deeper. She glances up at me and, from her expression, I am disgusting and will not ever be forgiven. Her son's throat twitches, as do his fists, and I know that if he were alone he would not be leaving, not be leading her gently away, he would be teaching me some of the lessons that women should learn. That and I'm beneath his dignity as a target. I'm like an animal making animal noises at him – scary at first and then a bit absurd and not a problem.

The last thing I can hear the mother say is, 'I shall have nightmares.' And whoever was holding my arm has increased the pressure. And I have just noticed, I've run out of words. I was supposed to be the good person involved here, but I've given someone's mother nightmares – the human mother of a human son.

They look exactly like people as they leave and I am exactly like people as I stand and stare after them. That is supposed to be what keeps us together: that we are the same, the same amount of stupid and angry and clever and tender and fine. The three of us, we're people, after all, the same thing, the same terrible thing.

What's left of the crowd around the enclosure is quiet as stopped clocks. It concentrates on being interested in everywhere I am not. It is being polite, in the sense of being deaf and blind.

I turn and see it's a youngish man who's still holding my arm. He squeezes it once, reaching over with his free hand to emphasise the gesture, and then lets go. I don't know what he means by this. People don't always express themselves that well.

Distant, the son tells his mother, 'Well, that's your choice.' And his tone is peculiar, metallic.

After that I can't hear them, because they are too far away.

So I have nothing to do. I don't want to watch the gorillas any more because they seem too marvellous and gentle and therefore unlikely to prosper as a species. I don't want to stand up. I don't want to have this face and be this person. I don't want to be thirsty. I don't want to have missed the choughs.

The young man leaves without doing anything further. I watch while what was left of the gorillas' original audience scatters and thins: one set of people effortlessly changing into another. Eventually I am surrounded by human beings who are simply staring at apes and not being repulsed by anyone.

This is when I suppose that I have to leave, too. I vaguely expect that I have been reported by someone for something, although I'm not sure of what. I walk off in a direction that I think I haven't tried yet and my feet feel worried, unreliable.

It is difficult to swallow, in part because of the thirst, and there are no choughs, and back at his house, Mort is no longer there and was never my uncle, was always more, and if I walk down to the beach below his house I will not be younger.

And it seems that I have lived my way into an age when almost everything good is ending. That's sad for the lemurs and the ibises in the same way it is sad for us.

I sit on a bench until my pulse steadies. I close my eyes and breathe in leafiness, water, livingness, the faint tangs of exotic droppings, blossoms. I feel exhausted, but also washed. All this, all this, all this immediate reality, seems inward-rushingly extraordinary, perfect. The green, so many greens become insistent. The fancy ducks, the sun on pelts, the children who run and are unguardedly happy and who may stay that way – all of this is newly intense. And no one is shooting the animals, no one is killing anything here in this place, in this moment. No one is murdering anyone here today. Sometimes you can hold that, wind it between your fingers and feel all right.

In the end I do find the zoo's restaurant and drink some water and then some tea. I eat. I'm always out of sorts if I don't eat. No one points at me and announces that I am the mad and angry woman who made the fuss in front of the gorillas. I go to the Ladies and rinse my face, my human face, using my dextrous and evolved human fingers.

That evening, back in the house that is no longer his, I unwrap every one of Mort's presents to me. I receive them. He paid that lawyer to make sure I would. It's important to give each other things.

He gave me this – bequeathed me his Jersey Death Elaboration.

I travelled back on the ferry a few days later, having cleared the house. I had an extra bag full of gifts that were intended for someone I didn't quite manage to be.

And I did get to see choughs, eventually, in other places. I probably will see them again – I have time.

Mort's letters didn't mention choughs. He does talk about gorillas and the way they seem so melancholy.

As I explained in our last summer, their faces are made to be sad, but they are not unhappy. In this they are like some humans. Other humans are very unhappy, but try to seem glad. People do their best.

Am Sonntag

She kept on sleeping long after the daylight arrived. Nobody woke her.

And there is no shouting, no din of wooden shoes, no chaos.

She is in this big room, such an empty big room, and all alone. The peace feels like panic on her skin.

And while she slept the world proceeded. Sunheat lolled across the naked floorboards. The birds sang. They are singing now. A fly against one of the windows is trying to nail itself out through the glass and may have been doing this for hours: left window, right window, audibly beating its body against something hard that it can't understand.

With or without her all this would still be here. It's proof she isn't necessary, but she knew that anyway.

And somewhere far away there is a sound, intermittent, a noise she doesn't want to hear.

This new tall room is gentle, though. It holds the heat of early afternoon, also a table, one chair, a thing she doesn't like and this bed which is so very clean and so unlikely. She wants to rest here, surrender. It's just that apparently, long ago, she was turned into an urgent animal. They did that to her, made her feel always caught in a blank wide space that cannot hide her.

If she changes again, she doesn't know what she'll become.

By the far wall stands that thing – an empty metal clothes rail with wheeled feet: brass rods combining in sharp angles, forming a substantial frame to hold suspended weight. She can't be calm about the way it looks.

And the rail reminds her of the customary jokes, it has their taste: giving a clothes rail to a woman with no clothes.

She came here in borrowed things, given things, found things. They must have once been worn by other people. She didn't enquire where the other people were. No one sensible does. In her clothes which had fitted limbs and bodies more substantial than her own, she had ridden in a truck that smelled of gun oil, metal and male boredom. Last night, the truck brought her here, finally a peaceful place like here. A woman with tired eyes had led her upstairs in swinging lamplight and then briskly left her beneath a bare electric bulb. The windows then were slabs of inquisitive darkness. She had waited, stood and waited, tried to think. This had lasted possibly for hours, before she had allowed herself to undress, crouching in the corner by the door for modesty. She had folded her latest costume over the lonely chair, rolled each stocking and put one in each shoe, set them neat on the floor. She didn't want to use the clothes rail or go near it, especially not at night. The bulb is still pointlessly burning overhead. She hadn't felt able to switch it off.

But the chair is safe, is clearly kind. It's the bentwood type you might see in a café: those bentwood chairs with wicker seats and live bodies sitting on them and talking about how the newspapers are dismaying. Hats tilted back and broad, happy gestures and aren't politicians eternally disappointing and isn't each side of each question much the same and isn't it best to stay reasonable and calm? There are terrible people always, of course, and parades to display and placate them, and there are nights full of rival thugs fighting in the streets, but the worst of that must be done with. The pendulum swings into pain and fear and darkness, but surely its furthest extreme is precisely what pushes it back. The propaganda sheets are loud and lurid, but no one of any intelligence will read them. All is in order beneath the passing rages.

Cafés make you have faith in civil stability.

But the monsters like cafés, as well.

That intruding sound continues, beating up softly through the house from somewhere below. She hopes she doesn't have to recognise it. She would prefer that.

She remembers their café instead, calls it back carefully, slowly.

Blue warmth on a Sunday morning and coffee and hot rolls, sugar, butter, honey, jam and nobody understanding how remarkable that is. Brushing hands while you ask for more, knowing there is more, and you gossip, complain about prices. Everyone is more furiously jolly the worse it gets, because what else can one do? And you tell the latest jokes designed to really bring the big men down to size. Cake and cigarette smoke and young leaves overhead, soft as green liquid, sparrows who chirp like tiny hammers against stone, who are eager for crumbs.

Everyone used to sit out in the open, where they could be seen, where anything could happen. On Sundays they might even motor right up to the lake, or else take the train from Zoo Station, then walk out under the trees beyond the villas to the cool, lazy water, step down into it. Brushing hands that gleam with water, being vehemently happy to spite it all.

The braced curves of the chair are still intact and they are more than she can bear.

It is sensible to stay away from beauty, because it summons up its own destruction. She was taught how it draws attention: that dancer who wore his hair long, that cabaret comedian who made those remarkable, outrageous flourishes of words, ladders and towers that could reach up to anyone, that girl with the green velvet coat and not a mark on it – they all faded away. You never do want to have anyone's attention.

It must have been well past midnight when she arrived. And her tiredness was quite different here and her undressing was quite different here and the close of the door with her inside was so different, so different, so wonderful.

She washed herself before bed in what seemed a paradise bathroom and took so much time about it, a life's worth. The water in the bath was grey after, only grey. She let it out, made it run away, and then wiped down the porcelain with a towel, the big one that someone had left at the foot of her bed. By the time she had finished polishing, rubbing, cleaning, she was dry.

She didn't look in the mirror.

She isn't going to look in a mirror.

The bathroom-wall tiles were a colour which is, which is, which is called *eau de Nil* and everything else was so perfectwhite, remains perfectwhite like something you'd find in the house of a living person in an ordinary time.

She still smells of what she assumes was American soap. They have everything now. But when she brushed her teeth – they gave her a new toothbrush, tooth powder in a tin – when she brushed her teeth last night, when she spat – the taste was still in her, the stink of where she came from.

How long it will hide in her is unclear. How long it will hide in her makes a cold pressure burst at the back of her neck. She doesn't scream. She never screams.

By the bed there's an old glass carafe, milky blue and complete. It's filled with water, sitting on the floor, crowned with a worn tumbler, the shine of the surface worried away. She can reach down and pour this water, drink it whenever she wants.

In fact, she does. Because she can. She drinks it all, this clean water.

This is being thirsty on the standard, human scale, a tiny need.

The water and the bed, the sheets holding her skin in softness, they help her to forget about the clothes rail. A person might come and use the clothes rail, people might come, people will come, people always come. People always came.

People came and hit Laszlo in the face. They threw him down steps and his spine broke.

When you sit in the summer air outside a café and hear sparrows and eat bread, you don't know how little it takes to break your spine. You have no idea. You can assume that you know your country's heart, not consider leaving, assume it's your home.

Even so, you stop telling jokes in case somebody hears them.

She remembers that new jokes won: the kind about dying to the sound of polkas and laughing while the dogs lunge in, the kind about the joy in practised motions with familiar implements. Only certain people had the right to smile.

After that things happened faster, so many people running for so many reasons. And they took her name away. No matter what she would stare at the gabardine, the boots and not the faces. She learned that – to never lift her eyes. She learned to hope each new place smelled of bedbugs, because then it would be warm.

But it's warm here and it's clean here and she is lying in white sheets and there is no more gabardine.

The clothes which are not her clothes but only a series of incidents, they shouldn't be on the chair, they shouldn't touch it. The past will stink in them forever. They ought to be burned.

Her breathing rises, rises and she makes herself still, holds on to the edges of the mattress, digs her fingers in and wishes herself unremarkable, unchallenging, translucent. In the end this would never have saved her, but it did work for a while, for long enough.

And there is no blood here, no shit, no piss, no dirty rags concealing.

Concealing.

There are no skeleton madmen here, jerking and stiff-legging inwards towards you and stealing everything, saying words that have no meaning but still make you run.

Concealing.

She watches the dust motes turn and glint in the light pealing down from the windows. The sound breaks in again, it beats.

It is the noise pianos make.

But it can't be.

She knows that people are always waiting to kill other people, take what they like, do what they like. They wait until somebody finds the right key and turns it for them, unlocks murder. She knows being able to walk is more important than food, water, money, photographs, and so that must govern what you carry with you. She knows that whatever you have will be taken in any case. She knows that inside herself, under skin, she is filthy, a terrible grease on her bones. But that is the sound of a piano. She knows that, too.

The notes rising up to her are sweet in the way that blossom would be sweet: high, flawless clots of scent and colour. They're sweet as the feel of a hand closing around your finger.

Before she can realise it she is standing, she is pummelling and twisting her way into those counterfeit clothes, the ones that leave her fumbling to find unfamiliar pockets.

The idea of *piano* lets her go to the left-hand window and stand, stare out at a lawn which lies perhaps two storeys beneath her. It has the kind of velvet turf which shows it is long-established and gently sinks towards a gleam of water, a silk expanse. Here and there are the ghosts of invaded flower beds and thick explosions of unregulated life. A far shore is visible, a riverbank, a lakeside, which is clothed in woods. There is only one space among the trees, a rough circle of empty earth, charred and shattered branches.

Near the edge of the lawn there are people, there are the moving bodies and heads of people who are alive and playing in the water. The upwards burst of their shoulders, their bodies when they stand is not distressed. Their outlines are distorted by sun spatters and glints, but she can see that they have brown and easy limbs. They wade, they make unforced gestures of no importance, they swim.

There are little boats.

There are bodies lying on the grass, lying on blankets, but they are reading books, talking, laughing, breathing.

And there is a piano.

She tries to persuade her throat, her lungs, her hands, that nothing bad is happening. She concentrates on gently and quietly noticing the blue-painted table in the centre of the wide room. On the table is a tin alarm clock. The clock ticks gently like a metal hen pecking at endless abundance.

Each of the notes is repeated, three times, four times, and as it repeats it bends, becomes correct, and then is left behind in a slow progression through the octaves.

Somebody is tuning a piano. So many things would be needed for this to exist, so much civility between strangers.

Although she is nervous of large buildings because of what they can contain she walks to the door barefooted and opens it, goes outside into a corridor. In daylight it is clearly elegant, but also slightly battered, tired. Objects have been dragged along the walls, left smears and gouges.

The notes rise to her, slightly louder.

Blood shifts, swings in her skull, but she keeps on. It's so odd to walk now as her body alters, decides if it will strengthen, continue. Her legs are stiff, weak. Inside her jacket pocket is a stone. It is a stone from somewhere else which she has brought here. She no longer has a religion. She has the stone.

The corridor leads past closed doors, she must think of them as harmless doors, and then turns, leads her to a generous sweep of steps, a plunging stairwell and a skylight overhead. She could jump here and create a splendid gesture. She could jump here and kill herself now that nobody else can.

This must have been a lovely villa: cut flowers and servants, tea served under leaf shade on the lawn. Then this must have been appropriated: everything lovely was stolen eventually, beauty that caught attention.

She pads down the broad wooden stairs, lower and lower, moves carefully, for fear of offending.

She sinks to the next level where the stairs reveal another passage and more doors. And here is a child, a childachild, a girlchild, and here this girl child is sitting. She is hunch-shouldered in a dirty green dress and bare feet, too, this girl. She is alone. When she lifts her face it is a dull, small emptiness.

The girl drops her gaze back to the naked floorboards between her outstretched legs, begins running her fingers along the spaces between the planks.

Then a far door opens, as if it has felt that a stranger is near, and a thin man steps out. She moves like someone pushing herself through water. He says something which isn't angry and has soft consonants, aiming at the child.

Then the man wags his hands and makes the shapes of being innocent and being not there. He goes to the girl, performing apology and fear, and then halts beside what may be his daughter, his daughter. He sits down in clockwork stages. The child ignores him. His folds his arms and produces this low moaning, which grows louder as he stares at a space in mid-air.

The girl pays no attention.

Perhaps because of the girl's fingers, or the presence of useless emotion, burned-out emotion, the lines between the floorboards appear to gather speed in some manner, to threaten.

The corridor becomes aggressive, swaying. It presses against her with damp heat.

She leaves the child and the man who may be a father, backs away, turns with a stumble, catches the handrail and regains the stairs. She can feel that her legs are trembling, that her body is twitching and perhaps her face.

She ought to be glad that a father and daughter have survived.

Instead, she hates them both. Her feet jar on the wood while she walks and she is furious with them both. Faster and harder than she means to she paces on towards an open landing that hangs out over an even broader curve of steps, makes a kind of long balcony.

Anyone could be tipped very easily over the bannister and down onto the mosaic tiles being pretty across the floor of the entrance hall. It would be too fast to prevent. The worst things always are.

The air tastes suddenly filthy, obscene, reeks of the place where they took her name. If it weren't for the piano sound, she would suffocate, although the space around her is high, proud, expansive, designed to imply the force of wealth.

Wealth didn't save you. It was worse than beauty.

She shakes her head to make her thinking go away and it turns her dizzy. She could fall herself, go out over the carved oak and metal, die without quite meaning it.

These final stairs are clearly intended to expose whoever walks on them to the gaze of those below. Although there is nobody watching this makes her sweat. There are no corpses lying across the mosaic. Nevertheless, her body is somehow preparing to run. The good sleep must have given her strength. She could get quite far.

Only the piano keeps her slow, each group of softly rounded notes getting louder, bumping against her, bursting.

She steps on to the tiles, feels the cool of them echoing upwards, pressing. At this lowest level there is the dusty smell of a warm old building and also distant kitchen noise. The air is being coloured with cooking: vegetables, clean bread. The living have to eat. They have to live. And she is so hungry and so ashamed of being hungry, of being able to be hungry. She swallows and swallows and swallows and steadies one hand against the wall.

Although she is terrible and ashamed, she permits the piano to call her, bring her into the swaying space, three storeys of nothing beginning to flex above her. She moves past the huge central table with its monumental vase, holding a bright shout of wild flowers. Beneath it she can see a tumble of worn boards and boxes: children's games. They almost halt her.

Set against panelling to her right is a noticeboard: unfamiliar images, quiet ink. Nothing about it is trying to kill anyone.

On the left is a terribly open door, but the room beyond is only filled with battered armchairs. Figures sit here and there in silence and she looks away from them for fear of needing to recognise a face, the line of a back, some tiny sight of something.

A muscular front door is propped open and gives sight of a grey stone balustrade, bow-fronted steps like frozen stages in a liquid advance and then a sleeping garden, a broad approach of mossy gravel, gates. A bicycle dozes on its side beneath a tree. It could indicate fight and struggle, but seems not to.

She ought to be checking now for routes she might take between the shrubs, for cover, gaps in hedges, fences, chances to overcome walls. Instead she keeps on walking inside the sounds from the piano. The notes aren't far away now, they have the strength to cut her open.

And here it is – the high, dark doorway, its threshold framed in gold-veined and complacent wood. She goes in, there's no helping it.

And, my God, my God, a grand piano, shining like a still, deep pool, like moonlight.

The room tastes of unending summers, habitual polish, a trace of decay. Walls and ceiling are panelled in more of this dully glowing timber. Close the door and you'd be shut up in a box.

The dead are gone, it's the living who can't rest.

And the piano. Flawless.

The man sitting at the keyboard looks at her. He might have been waiting, he might have expected that she would have to come, to see, to come, to see the cloth roll of innocent implements, tuning fork, tuning hammer, the wedges, the temperament strip, his ways to summon sharp of pure and flat of pure and make all right, in order.

The man has pushed his glasses up to rest over his forehead, just exactly the way that a living man might. White hair, old suit, twisted hands. He's still looking at her with sky-blue eyes. The collar of his pale blue shirt gapes round his neck.

And she knows about setting the temperament, pure and wide of pure. She knows how the strands of a sound will spread, that a tuner must make all parts of a note agree and be in order. For the human ear to understand it, each sound must be not unmercifully true, but only true enough for people and the world.

The piano is a beautiful compromise, the wires collaborating.

Piano wire can hang you. They were sure to discover that, try to make it a violent thing.

Ugliness makes more ugliness so that it can feel at rest.

She hears her voice making noises that aren't words.

The man at the piano swallows, nods to her, keeps looking into her eyes, as if this will be a solid point for them while everything else sweeps away. Then he sets his hands above the keys.

She understands that if he plays she will probably die, but she wants so much to hear music again, to hear that music again.

And he begins.

At first he is tentative, explores, and then he plays flourishes and ladders, towers of notes to test the instrument.

And then she remembers: Judit, Ágnes, Alain, Simon, Ilona, Gustav, Max, Károly, Franz, August, Albert, Dora, Alma, Herta, Robert. She remembers.

For a while she can't hear any more, perhaps because she is louder than the music.

Anna, Paul. Anna. Anna.

But she isn't dying.

She feels the brush of Paul's hand in the café, in the crowd, in the speed and the din on the ramp and the air fills her mouth with the taste of human fat, but no one could know that would happen, you couldn't know that because how could anyone think that?

She still can't die. She can think of her mother taking Anna, being practical, because grandmothers and children won't be working outside, will have light duties.

Rushing away. Everything gone before you have words for it.

She isn't dying.

And the man is playing the piano like a living man and she doesn't know the melody and he makes it ring up as if he owns it, made it, kept it with him through all this.

He is alive, he is still playing, he exists, the music exists.

The way that he leans and sways, the press and dip and stroke of his fingers – it all means that she can't forgive him for not being Paul.

And when the melody touches her face, her fingers, when she breathes it in, it is the sound of still being alive when nobody else is.

Her husband is gone. Her daughter is gone. Her mother is gone. Such a great beauty, but it has no power to kill her, it can only tell her this, make her know and know and know this.

The man playing understands. He is still alive.

She is still alive.

It will be terrible, this surviving.

It Might Be Easier to Fail

You don't know when he's home, so that's a problem. He might have just popped out to make a speech, record a statement, remind himself he's relevant. And trying an action when he isn't there and couldn't notice, well, what would be the point? I'll only get one crack at him, most likely, and I wouldn't want my effort gone to waste. There has been too much waste.

I know he's not in charge any more, but guilty's guilty. I did consider other targets. He's the one, though. He's stayed relevant for me.

You can't do terrible things and not be punished. I'm saying that, writing that, thinking that, because saying and writing and thinking are always the start of a thing becoming true out in the world. You build the start of every alteration out of words. Whatever you do, good or bad, you'll have thought it first, named it first.

And there are so many things you have no power to alter – that means you have to mend the things you can. It doesn't make up for all of the things you can't alter, but it helps. That's why I'm making plans. I'm going to show him the truth he's been avoiding. I will be an example.

I've checked out the lie of the land. They guard the house while he's abroad, but not so much. When he's living in town, two coppers stand out at the nearest corner of the square. They're not just defence, they're a grandiosity, his kind of luxury item. Sometimes there's another couple in the alley behind the house and then there's the obvious pair at the top of the steps, up at his front door leaning about. Whenever the great man's overseas, a lad can be stuck on the door or at the corner by himself.

These would be the observations made to date. I was never military, but it's only common sense. They're saving money by dialling security down when he's far away, but this makes it very obvious when he's back, when he could be inside, when he could be on the point of walking out and down the steps, across the pavement.

I swing by at all hours, take in the scene, and then I get the next bus home. It's a bit of a long trip to get there, out of my way, and I have to change buses twice, so the journey gives me space for contemplation. I'm glad of it. For a while I couldn't think at all, not anywhere, couldn't be at rest. I painted the flat, repainted, built a wall in the garden out the back, then tore it down. The neighbours were worried, but I was acting logically. I wanted to be worn out, so I could sleep.

I find it very peaceful on the bus – top deck and looking out if I can manage. The idea that I'm recovering and have purpose will make me smile as passengers come and go. Some of them smile back. This means I've learned, because of the planning, that friendliness still happens maybe one time out of ten.

Free-range smiling in London is risky, of course. You can seem to have a strange agenda if you grin. But some people recognise innocence when they see it and they answer your smile. More smiling, that's a benefit, that's a small positive change made by my journeys. Knowing that gives me strength, while I try to work out what I'll do and how I'll do it.

Even the cops, when they see me now, they smile. I'm so regular they must think I'm a local. As if I could afford to live round here. I wear a Crombie coat that I found in a second-hand shop. I only bought it for the plan, so when it's on me I feel different, like a better man, like a secret man.

The cops always look as glum as Monday morning when they're stood by themselves: bulletproof vest and riot boots, machine gun and a sad, sad face. If a man's in the street and he's holding a machine gun, I'd generally prefer him to look cheerful. Him having a gun is serious enough. Even when they're standing with a pal, the cops seem gloomy. Bored, I suppose. You'd run out of things you could tell to each other: your mutual days and seasons and confessions sliding by and then repeating and in the end your better option's silence. Longer than some marriages, all those hours you'd spend together, exposed to the elements. *Good morning. Good morning, back. How'd you sleep? All right, thanks – how about you? Well, look at the rain. Yes, I've noticed it's raining – I'm standing underneath it right beside you. Well, there's no need to get shirty.* And so forth.

I'd like them to chat more, stay cheerful. I want them distracted by a happy partnership. Apply too much friction, too much grief to any relation, and the whole thing breaks up skywards – nothing you can do.

I had too much grief for my marriage to last, I'll admit that. She said I was obsessive, but that's wrong. I had no purpose, was my problem and I've fixed that. Trying to make my plan work gives me focus, lets me sleep. There's no obsession. For a while I would try to explain myself and get her to see, but it didn't work. You never should return and mess about once someone's lit their fuse. In the end she left and that was fair enough. I'd stopped really being with her. I'd stopped really being anywhere.

That's maybe why I love the buses – they're an intention, not a place. And they're part of the plan they're helping.

On the actual day, though, I'll have to walk a good deal, because the small hours would be best and most of the buses don't run then. Still, the small hours are quieter, they're sleepy and they're dark. I'd stand out more then, would be the problem. I'd be walking in and out alone.

When I pass through the square, I never do have the impression the cops are on high alert. They don't exactly sweep their surroundings with implacable vigilance. Not so as you'd notice. But I realise their demeanour might just be a pose. They'll be aiming to keep the public nice and calm, after all – *Oh, it's just Bill and Ben the security men with their friendly automatic weapons.* They may be tempting threats into taking them for granted. Then again, they may be pondering whether they'll have chips for their tea, composing poems, comparing the merits of various goalkeepers. I'm not sure how ready they'll be, how preoccupied. I can't tell what people think. The newspapers make suggestions, but I don't believe them any more.

The newspapers love my target. They let him still be a figure, man of influence.

On some days I completely assume that the coppers who guard him are mainly bored – that's what I feel. I chat to them – the couples and the solitary sentries – and they seem very glad that I've arrived. They also have this attitude about them that suggests – *Well, don't blame us. We don't want to be here, but it's our turn. We'd leave him and let him discover how he would do without our love, if we could choose to.*

They wouldn't mention love, but watching and checking, defending – they're all ways of showing love.

They're not disrespectful about him out loud, not exactly, but you see it in them. Their tone is ironic, implies that it's all some kind of joke: their being tooled up for urban warfare. He'd like that. He liked the firepower options, the torture options, knowing that he could hide anyone, cause them secret pain. He sent chaos out in the world and chaos is like hate – it always gets tired and comes back home.

The lack of respect his guards show him makes me like them, even though they're in my way. They'll half wink and give out a shrug as if they've been ordered to wait with their guns and get stared at while guarding a dog turd. They make sure you know they've done better and will do again. This could be wishful thinking on my part.

If I turned up wearing a T-shirt with a slogan, picketing with a placard, calling his name – any of that – they would still arrest me, I'm sure. The story afterwards would be about me and how I'm unreliable in my head. I don't want that.

I don't hate them. I don't hate him. You always want to keep away from hate.

I suppose he doesn't give the coppers much attention, or not enough to see their attitude. He's a man to make assumptions, because his kind always are, and he'll assume they'll always be there, serving him.

I talk with them about the weather, other leaders, one of them goes birdwatching at the weekends so we chat about that. Brief back and forths, nothing unprofessional. Their hands are so casual and rest so gently on those machine guns. You almost want to study their fingers with undue attention, in case one might absently curl against a trigger, let loose a few dozen rounds without warning. They could catch you in the legs by accident, quick as a sneeze or a giggle. A laughter-related injury.

If you've got a gun, you'll want to fire it – what else is it for?

He knew that and knows it still and takes advantage.

It may have occurred to the policemen – as it has, of course, to me – that if this man they're guarding really is what he says he is – a darling of the people and peacemaker between nations – then it is a touch peculiar that he needs the loaded weapons and dark skills there to defend him. You might start believing we're not all fond and grateful and that he knows it in his little heart. You might guess that he's sometimes afraid of what he's done – not scared enough to admit it, but still uneasy. Why would a man who's three-quarters of a saint, if not a whole one, be so keen to keep the loving world at bay?

The world isn't loving, I know, not all the time. The thing is that you shouldn't help to make it worse.

The newspapers tell me we miss him, or at least that we ought to take his wise advice as if he is our ever-tender father and knows best. I don't think that and neither do the cops.

Don't get me wrong, I know if I headed for the steps to reach his door, the police would respond. They smile and make weather-related remarks, but they'd kill me if they thought they ought to.

Unless they really are entirely tired of him. I sometimes dream they'd only watch as I trotted up and knock-knock-knocked and looked into the gloss of his big door, pressed the intercom.

In a kind world they'd glance at me, then stroll away, head down to the main road and maybe buy some dates, some halva, apples, milk. They both could find they had an errand that was pressing. It should be that only good leaders are kept safe. One drop of blood spilled and no one ought to shield you, not any more. That would mean the cops would leave me be until I'd done all I wanted. They would have examined my face and seen my innocent intentions. More people ought to think of this as a possibility. It would help a world that's trying to be kind. People, so many people, keep on being kind and gentle when nothing around them has been either one, not for years and years. He can't see that. We're not in his kind of houses, we're out in the streets where he can't go. Not him, not his wife and not his kids can walk two hundred yards and buy a paper. Not without security. The level at which he operates, it's like fame – he can't do anything for himself, by himself. And I suppose that might feel to him as if he's special, that might be like – *Here I am with staff, forever. I've made it. I can behave as if I am a toddler, or disabled, geriatric – rely on getting care and care and care. I needn't do anything that I don't want to, not ever again. No one can touch me, no one can get through.*

When normal things and people make you feel besieged that isn't normal. You end up at war. I meet people like that all the time now, they're inside a personal war they've declared against people they've never met, ideas they can't get the hang of, facts that hurt their feelings.

He didn't like facts, didn't listen to them. That's how you make mistakes. And he didn't like people. That's how you get cruel. He's like the rest of them who want to be in charge, who are in charge – they don't like anyone they haven't met. Their idea of who we all are is terrible, we make them scared, and somewhere inside they all know they're not marked for glory, not in a real way, they're not a celebrity, a star. They know we can see they're only freaks and so they hate us. He can't relax unless he's with his minders, with his warders, or with other golden shits. He thinks that's what success should feel like.

I could be wrong.

But if I'm right then I'm sorry for him, I truly am. A prison that you're proud of still keeps you locked up. He'll never face a court, never hand himself in, never set that kind of precedent, but you're still locked up, still under house arrest.

He'll have doctors and specialists, maintenance: he'll have his own team of people always there to make sure death can't creep inside and meet him.

Except death's already made itself at home. That's nothing to do with me, that's just reality and I'd want him to know about it, that he'll die, too. Death's a part of everybody's mechanism, inside and ticking away. That's why there's got to be a lot of kindness. Loving gets really needful when you start giving death some thought. I'd go into schools and give talks about it, I'd volunteer to explain that we want love to set a balance against the unfairness of death coming in like water, always finding a possible path. It's none of your business and on its way, so your focus should rest on the helping, because otherwise you'd drive yourself insane. You can't be permanent, no one can be permanent.

Kids would understand that, if I spoke to them. I'm good with kids. I tell them that kindness is your business in a proper life.

I want him to understand, too. The first heartbeat that someone doesn't get, the one when they don't join in with you in any more and there is silence ever after – if he knew how it felt to be there when death happens it would change him. I think it would change him.

That's why I thought I should demonstrate. At first I had no idea how.

I had no one I could discuss it with, not any more, no one to tell me I'm a fool. I miss that. Being told you're a fool is useful information, you can hold on around it and set to work.

When I'm in bed and awake and it's starting to be the sunrise – I call myself a fool then. I lose faith. There's light seeping up and it's irreversible and sleep won't come back and there's time on your hands – and you know that time is always about death and so you don't start well. It's easy to let yourself lose hope.

When that happens I concentrate on my message, how to make it clear. And how I decided that it should be blood, I ought to communicate with him using blood.

If he was to come outside and walk on the pavement and it was all blood then he might have to hear me. For a beat of his heart, he might be unsteady and that's a start. Blood is a shock.

Everyone acts and believes along tracks, over and over. Some people when they see where they've gone wrong, they'll change their routes. Some people are stuck. They're under house arrest inside their heads and nothing you tell them will make any difference. Nothing that you do can set them free. They have to feel a shock that hurts their soul, they have to know that it's their fault – that's when they get different, when they get brave enough to try.

I'm not guessing about this, I know.

Blood changes everything, so I'm going to show him blood.

Not poppies, not petals, not symbols – spilled blood.

I want him to wake to it and feel it like a curse, like the working out of a natural consequence.

I dropped paint in my garden on bits of paving, while the neighbours watched. Oil paint would have lasted best, but you can't really get it any more. I used acrylic, mixed the colours to be right. Blood, when it's fresh, is too red to be true. It's shining, still gathering oxygen, trying to be useful.

But paint isn't enough, not to change him.

Then I wondered if I could wear bags of animal blood, if I could hide them in under my clothes. I was going to use bags, or water bottles filled with pig's blood, cow's blood, whatever I could get. I experimented. I bandaged a couple of reservoirs to my chest, threaded their drinking tubes out from my jacket's sleeves. I wanted to make such a burst of blood.

I bought pig's blood from a butcher, but I couldn't keep it liquid. Blood clots. Blood stiffens and darkens and cakes. It coats surfaces like varnish. Sometimes I can forget, but I do know that. Blood does what blood does and you can't argue with it, but you want to. He has to see it because it's the most real thing there is.

When you see it on the pavement it makes no sense and it can't be a part of the world, because this was never a thing that could happen, but it keeps on spreading anyway.

The blood is so fast and so thick and it makes you panic and here is this life that you love, here's this person you watch for and check for and should defend and you were only this tiny bit late at the school gates. You can see her standing and so she's come just a dab, just a few steps further on beyond the barrier than usual. This is your fault because you're late arriving. You rush down this last few yards and wish she had stayed in the school hall because it's raining, falling harder all the time. She's on the pavement drifting, gently drifting, you were buying her an apple, a bag of apples, because you had none left and they're good for her and part of making everything safe and that's why you're late and you can see her, you can still see her being alive. As you head down the road to the T-junction she is standing with her scooter which you never liked, only she loves it, so you allowed her to take it to school, your wife allowed her to take it to school, because then she'll be happy and that's what you want. You and your wife work shifts that pass each other and it's not ideal, but it means that one of you will always be here, always meet her at the gates. She scoots along beside you in the mornings, in the afternoons, or else you pull her and she stands on it and is lazy. No, she is not a lazy child. She scoots and she runs and she skips and you walk – you have the taller legs – beside her. And at the end of the day she comes back with your wife, she comes back home with you, she rides on her scooter with her one foot paddling her along and you tell her she is a beautiful swan in sandals. You tell her that. This doesn't make you like the scooter and you make sure she is never out by herself on it and you make sure that she promises she will never do anything with it near a road unless you're by her, right by her, unless you or your wife are by her. And that day – the day in question – she's not even on it, or messing about, or doing something wrong – she's right there and she's perfect and you're almost with her, you need only cross the road and she is doing nothing that she shouldn't, only looking at you, giving all her attention to you and moving a step or two further along the pavement and she's smiling and waving, she's waving to you, only then she sort of stumbles for no reason you'll ever be able to think of later. You'll never find out a reason, not in any nights. But still, she stumbles and the way that she's holding the handles of the scooter make her stumbling more complicated and the rain falls and she falls and the metal falls, the scooter tumbles, and you're so close to her, but not close enough to catch her, not close enough in any way that counts and her face is extremely clear and she was smiling before, but now she stops and seems worried, she's puzzled and worried and maybe she's hurt a little and she'll cry. That's what will go wrong. You are both expecting she'll skin her knees and land with a bump. It's possible you both share those ideas.

Then there's a van here, very fast.

Blue van. Plain blue van, like in a kid's book.

This is the van which nobody could find, which none of the other parents could quite recall. And I couldn't remember the number plate. And I spoke to some police, but they didn't have machine guns.

The van had no markings that I can remember and I didn't look at it enough, because I was looking at my daughter.

I wake up and try to think of it.

Blood is shock.

I couldn't see her at the end because the van was in the way, it was between us and then it was gone.

And the rain fell down and drowned us both and her blood was everywhere, her blood was touching me and I couldn't put it back.

Her face was still perfect, but worried.

I didn't want her to be worried.

Why should the last thing for my daughter be that she was worried? I used to ask my wife that, while she blamed me and was right to blame me. I was late and I didn't save our daughter.

Crying on the pavement with all the blood. I'm kneeling and I know I won't ever stand and there will always be her blood soaking warm through my trousers and here on my hands and I can't put it back and make it right.

I understand that.

And I understand there can't be a death which isn't like that, if you look at the whole of its truth. The dead are always children, they used to be children, they'll always be children, the rest is just details. And you can't ever drop a bomb, for fear of killing children. You can't ever fire a bullet, for fear of killing children. The only thing worse than death is to cause a death. It will destroy you.

I could have waited and then bought the apples with her, with her scooting along tight beside me, still beside me, still.

I want him to understand he is destroyed.

I picked him because the decisions he made killed children and this has destroyed him, but he's kept on moving and he has allowed more people to kill children and be destroyed. I think I can make him see this and when I have this will be the start of everybody seeing.

I want the meaning of blood to be completely clear. Morning after morning after morning, I want him to see the signs I've left him.

Morning after morning after morning, I want everybody looked after.

Morning after morning after morning.

I don't mean to do him any harm, but blood has to coat the pavement, to spread out and teach him. My own blood, I carry that with me. I'm not sure how quickly they'll stop me, or if I hold enough. It will be hard, but I won't fail. You have to make your suffering have meaning, or you're lost.

I've got love in my heart. That's important, that helps you win.

Morning after morning after morning, I've got love.

Point for Lost Children

Old ladies get away with things, they're fly.

She's getting away with loads, but I don't mind. She's sitting down with me here and we're chatting, kind of chatting, so nothing about us is causing any bother. That's her effect. She makes every mortal thing fine, like your gran did, or your aunties. My mum had all these sisters, household of women with her dad dead. Aunties all over the place while I was wee.

Get an old lady involved and you'll turn your whole situation, get it blessed, and you can see that she's wise to that. She's giving out the cheeky grin to everyone.

I could lean back, shut my eyes and imagine we're relaxed and in a café, one that we've chosen as our latest favourite place. Or maybe we're side by side and feet up in her living room with biscuits. Then we'd maybe attend some kind of display, demonstration, doing our best for community art. We'd be kind about it after.

We're sitting on the floor together, which you can't do in a café. In other places, though, it's usual. Sometimes you'll make yourself sit this way for health – it's practically yoga.

I can't do yoga because it hurts. I've my legs stuck out straight ahead, because anything else will mess me up.

We're not in a café, we're in a Tube station. They both have heating, which makes them the same in a way I like.

We're not friends, but we could be, we could end up that way. Mibbee pals. *Mibbee's aye, mibbee's naw* – nobody understands me if I say that. Only she might. She's listening and that's the way you get your ear in for kenning aw the way folk speak.

I could be someone who's fresh in her street and she's popped round like a friendly person to coorie in and say she's retired and handy for help. She'd find things out about me, but not in a bad way – old ladies do that, they get the skinny on a'body, every one. They get away with the curiosity – like Columbo.

My gran enjoyed Columbo because he was the wee guy and didn't seem smart, but in the end he'd sort the bad yins and get justice. Gran wanted to iron him and cut his hair, but she loved him, too – him with the one eye, but doing his best. There's a sympathy between old ladies and Columbo.

She walked right up to me with intention, as if we'd arranged to meet and finally seeing me had made her day. She leaned in and smiled and then sort of paused – like she was waiting to join with the chorus in some song she was thinking about – then she reached her right time and she sat. Her hip bumped against me while she wriggled her way down the wall, but not enough to do any harm. She's slow but more flexible than I'd expected. As she settled, she said, 'Budge up.'

I budged.

She asked, 'So how was this morning?' It was just as if we did this every day.

And you stop being used to questions and speaking and all that, because nobody lets you. You get this clot under your tongue instead of talk. Then even having a go makes you nervous. Or else, someone starts a conversation and they mean you to join in and you do and you've got all this stuff in your head that normally would get out, wee bit by wee bit, but it's this rush now, it's leaping out of you all at once. You end up scaring folk. They decide you're on the street because you're mental.

Mostly I just say thank you, because you can't go wrong with that. People enjoy being thanked.

For about a week, I tried Stay well. Be happy. Didn't work out.

I do my best, but it's no use most times. I'm made the way that's never any use.

This woman, she's saving me all of the bother of talking back. She's got information about the weather and government and the right ways to eat fruit and do I know about the nearest shelter, which I do know about the nearest shelter. I don't have the money to get in the nearest shelter, or any shelter, and I'm not allowed to ask for money, so I can't get into any shelter and I can't get a job to earn money because I'm not in a shelter, so I don't have an address, so being homeless makes me homeless – that's how it works.

It's funny how sometimes you get raging and it's with the wrong people. Folk will make you angry because they're being nice, but they can't help you. Only the people who hate you can help and they don't want to. The good folk think there'll still be a solution.

The woman's nice, she can't help it. And she's got a funny voice – high and higher and then it tumbles down. Pigeons do that, the way they fly. I watch them when I'm outside. They scramble up into the sky and then seem to surrender, they drop. Every time they make me wonder if they've died and given up. Makes me sick.

She doesn't mean to make me sick, but she still does.

Her eyes are a bit birdy – dark and searching about. She's like a garden bird, a park bird – something scaredy that gets hunted, not an eagle, or a hawk or any kind of killer like that.

She's off her head a bit, but in a kind way – she's not a bam. I see it a lot – everybody does – the way people's heads go and hit the ground when they start to get homeless. You see them smash out here. Being crazy makes whoever you were get bigger, clearer. You're in pieces, you're skelfs in a bag and out here – but if you're nice you get nicer. And the opposite. It magnifies the biggest part of what you are.

I think that's right.

I don't know what I am. I don't know what I'll be.

I keep steady, I think.

I count the steps that lead up to the street, count the feet that come down them and the ones that climb. If you're counting hard you can't think of anything else.

I tell the women I am skippering and then I translate myself – I am sleeping rough. I don't explain the way the shelters are, because the thought of them's making her happy. You can't sleep in them, you shouldn't. You're up all night counting everything to keep your head straight. To keep the heid. And the bams are being bams and the noise is awful and if you liked praying you'd try that. Nothing helps. Nothing keeps the shite at bay.

And you don't want it climbing inside you.

I tell her I'd like to be out in the country and by myself. I'd save up and get a caravan. I can't, but I say it anyway. I say I'd go away on a boat, my own boat. None of this is possible, but the woman doesn't say so.

I don't count out loud when I get the stress. I count in the quiet of my brain. She doesn't notice, no one does.

And I listen to her while she tells me about her morning. Her back is grumpy – she says *grumpy* with a smile, as if she forgives it for hurting her. She says that she's liking the start of the sunshine and that it is cheerful, or cheering.

I can't hear the end of her sentence, because I remember about needing water when it's hot. London in the summer's trying to kill you, every time. You can't bear it.

I start counting the buttons on jackets as they go by me. This is risky, because sometimes people pass too quickly and I don't get the numbers right. Missing numbers frighten me.

I know that makes me seem like a mentalist, but I'm not. I definitely know an awfy, awfy, terrible thing is never going to happen because I've messed up my totals. Terrible things happen, but not because of that.

It's just that my body believes in the numbers and thinks it will die and then it doesn't want to breathe, because corpses don't need to.

I used to have a therapist. She was good.

Now I onetwothree.

The people with the jackets would rather not see me. They'd all rather I was away. They're thinking I'm a junkie, alky, junkie, alky. Their faces say that. They're going to think the old lady is that way, too. I don't want to infect her, but I do.

I try to find something to count on her clothes.

She has these extendable walking poles, one for each hand, like she's going to explore a mountain, later on.

I can't count a pair. A pair takes no time. I still like her, even so.

Big daft orangey skirt, she's wearing, with a big daft orangey shirt flopped over it and on top is a long red waist-coat. So many layers would make her a bundle if she was plump, but under it all you can guess that she's wiry.

I tell her she looks like a Tibetan monk, or a Tibetan monk's mum.

I've forgotten how to make a joke work and maybe this isn't one and maybe I'll offend her.

I count her fingers and then count mine. We're almost the same colour – the outside colour. Hers is because she wants it. Hers is to do with being healthy.

Then she giggles, presses her elbow against my ribs, not too hard.

So I haven't messed up.

The woman, she's making me feel brave – risk a joke. I used to be all full of courage. My therapist helped. And she taught me meditation. I attended Taoist classes for t'ai chi. I learned the whole form. The teacher said we were moving the way a brave person moves in the world. I had a wee greet at that – cried – but she pretended she didn't notice.

I used to do that – the self-care. I was moving forwards.

When they assessed me the last time, I told them about the t'ai chi, but only to say that I'd had to stop, because of the panic attacks coming back and the pains in my shoulders. That isn't what they wrote down on my papers.

They lie. Whenever they assess you they always lie.

I was married and he lied, my man. His lying felt the same – and the way they take everything from you. That felt the same. I ended up by myself with him, because he took me to his city and away from my life. He told me things until I believed them. He was always certain and kept on. He told me who I was and it was terrible and I gave up. You've got no energy by the finish and you give up. It's pathetic.

I count the lace holes on the woman's trainers.

Bouncy white trainers she has and scarlet hair in what is called a Page Boy Cut, which I used to have once. Her hair must be naturally white because the dye job's magic, perfect. It makes her look dead futuristic.

She says that she looks like a gonk and I think that's sad, because it means she hates herself and I start wondering who made her do that, only then she grins and tells me that gonk hair is what she's aiming for.

When I was in Primary 5 gonks were what you collected. That's how old I am – I go back to gonks and toys that existed and weren't online. Tablets were something you took, then. I lined my gonks along my windowsill. The daylight faded their colours, but I didn't mind and didn't think it bothered them. I had more than anyone. At school I was the kid type of famous because of them.

She's talking about something being a sin. She's patting my arm and nodding her red, red head. I don't think she's religious.

I sat once outside a shop and over the road these people in suits were giving out Christian leaflets. A man stopped and shouted at them – straight into shouting, no conversation – and then he pointed at me. He made me scared. I was going to get myself gathered up and moved away, before he did anything to me. He crossed between all this bealing traffic, crossed the road at a run, and gave me a tenner. I didn't get the money because I was me, I got it because he was angry with the Christians, but that didn't matter.

I had a lovely childhood. Before all this. I had wonderful times and the aunties gave me money – Christmas and birthdays. Not much, but a lot for a wean, a child. I saved up. I'm not here because I don't know how to save. I'd rather the woman could think about that than be sorry for me.

Slung over the woman's body, she's got a cloth bag and it looks like it's Indian, or something. It's got countable wee mirrors all over it. I'd been saving them up until later, but I'm getting right intae them. The embroidery's keeping them safe and anchored, which makes them feel good, when you onetwothree.

I would like her to be secretly a warrior with kung fu skills. She'd be ladylike, but still cowp you on your arse and leave you out cold if you were a bastard.

This is too difficult to explain.

I want her to move the bag so I can see more mirrors.

T'ai chi is martial art, but also peaceful. It prepares you, so you'll never have to fight, because you're different in the world and so the bastards pass you by. The bams try it on with other people who aren't you and can't see your weakness.

I miss it, making the movements, having Beautiful Lady Hands.

Your courage drains away.

The woman's still brave, you can tell. And she's dead hippy so her name ought to be Sky, or River. She could be Isthmus, Archipelago – something geographical.

I have Higher Geography. I could put that on a card at my feet.

I did O grades and then Highers – they were the qualifications in Scotland at the time. I got Higher History, Maths, English, Biology and Geography. I don't have my certificates any more, but there must be records. I heard it's different now, but we had Sixth Year Studies after Highers. You had to write a dissertation, which was meant to be good practice for uni.

I never got to uni and it wasn't good practice for anything important. They were a pish certificate. Folk stared at you about them in interviews and there you'd been, trying your best.

I've learned things. I don't get to prove it, but some of the stuff must be in there, still. I learned how to move like somebody who's brave and I could have gone to uni. Marrying Billy happened, though, instead. It was very fast. Then you're stuck. We were meant to have kids but I couldn't which was probably the start of it going wrong.

I tell her I'm Anne.

I'm still Anne.

The woman says that she's called Marilyn, which isn't geographical. It's a glamorous name to give your daughter.

Marilyn's face lets you know that she's mature, but being embracive about it.

Embracive sounds like I made it up.

Marilyn is embracive.

Marilyn has wooden buttons on her waistcoat – one-twothreefourfivesix – sixfivefourthreetwoone.

We had a tin of buttons at home when I was wee: wooden and tortoiseshell and horn and glass and pearl and toggles and fancy ones and the woven leather kind for cardigans.

I was going to make my own tin later. A home isn't only furniture and somewhere to have a bath, or pillowcases in a stack that smell of your wash and being looked after in your sleep. Your home has to have foolishness, as well. Saving up buttons is practical, but you can run your fingers through them for the feel as well – the sound and the feel and how you count them – that makes happiness.

The button tin is for you and whoever you love and for when you have kids. You're expecting to have a life and so you get a tin and start to fill it.

Marilyn will have a tin. She's the type to make her details nice and to seek enjoyment. She seems as if she tries to like everything at least a bit for the whole of the time she's awake. She'll enjoy sleeping as well, it won't upset her.

I talk to her about being a girl and running my fingers and swimming my fingers in the buttons and I am expecting that she'll laugh, but instead she says her daughter was called Abby. That means her daughter's in the past.

When she headed for me, she met my eyes and her face said I would be the next thing she'd enjoy. I've made her sad instead.

It was in my papers that talking to strangers is difficult for me. When you get your assessment, that's with a stranger. If you don't go then they take all your money away. But when you go you're proving you can deal with strangers and that's part of how you ruin all your hopes. In the room where the health professional put me there wasn't enough to count. I asked if I could tip the paper clips out of their box. I take paper clips with me. They said that was a threat. That was me wanting to throw paper clips and be nasty.

Wanting to kill myself wasn't a threat.

Safe now, though.

I'm safe.

I've got all the wee mirrors to count and they're shining and happy.

Marilyn's here and we are sitting together, sitting on the floor together in Leicester Square Underground Station and we're getting away with it. That's Marilyn's triumph, that's a sign of her power.

All this should be wonderful, but she's sad. The sad is getting into my sweatshirt and then into my arm where she's resting against it.

She is telling me about her daughter and I am nodding, but I'm making this big effort not to hear, because it's going to be a very bad story. She'll have tried her best and her best won't have done enough.

I keep nodding.

And I'm just sitting, not begging. I'm being company for her – I haven't asked Marilyn for anything.

No one's allowed to give money to anyone inside the Underground. They make announcements saying that. They tell folk to give their money to the charities instead. I tried with the charities, but I'm still waiting, because they don't have the money, so I'm here, where I can't get the money for myself.

We're sitting like pals. She's telling me things that only pals tell each other. Then she'll feel better, because she's strong.

I really would like her to be strong – otherwise it's going to get black in my head. That won't be her fault and she doesn't mean it, but it will happen anyway.

Yes, she's powerful and I bet she has younger chums, the age of me. I bet she takes an interest in women who haven't flowered yet and need coaxing out into the world. I know that she's looking for daughters, doing what she can. I count, she looks for daughters, ones she can save.

And she'll be keen with them about canoeing, or going off hiking up hills with her poles and showing what can be done, demonstrating their potential. She could wander out across countries and stay safe, because she'll be honestly nice to everyone and the locals will keep an eye out on her behalf. When you're already doing all right, people will help you. Marilyn will think the world smiles a lot. That's because of who she is, though, not because of the world.

While she's away she can think Abby's back at home and the space between them's just geography.

I used to sit the park, away from Billy, and pretend I'd be going home to somewhere else. I'd imagine the furniture and hanging curtains.

I'd go up the mountains with her. I'd like to. We could head up to summits, boots going and the poles working away, and her other chums will be soft and breathless from hanging about at unis or going to clubs, or eating junk because their kids are young, or their lives leave them tired for other reasons and that's when you want to eat rubbish.

I mean, I couldn't climb a mountain now, but with Marilyn I would get stronger. We would walk round the nearest park and practise.

We won't.

I know that. It's just a good idea while I lean myself forward, keep a bit away from how she's unhappy and count her fingers and count mine and then repeat.

I started out in the prime of health.

I got those good Highers.

I could have done anything.

She won't stop telling me about her daughter. Abby went to clubs. Abby got lost in things. Abby had all of the love that there was, but she got defeated.

I don't want to know that. You're supposed to stay well if you've got love. There's nobody safe if that isn't true.

Abby got chemical.

Abby faded and ghosted away.

I'm not a junkie. I never went to clubs, or only for the dancing. I couldn't get enough of it. I wasn't that much to look at, never been bonny, but guys would take an interest when they saw me move. Then I'd turn them away.

Before Billy, I turned them all away. That's who I was, very free.

And Billy was honey and stars until you knew him, until he'd got you.

Onetwothreefourfivesixsixfivefourthreetwoone.

I tell her that Abby must have been in the clubs for dancing and gone wrong. I start to see Billy's face, Billy's face looking down when I'm caught on the floor, Billy's eyes full of his fix, his fresh fix.

Marilyn starts crying.

She puts her hands into her lap and folds fingers between fingers as if she is trying to be two people who are touching. I tilt my head and keep on tilting until I'm leaned against her shoulder.

The blackness is roaring out of her and into me, but I can't leave her lonely. She's like my pal.

Her hair smells of things that I cannae remember – can't – they're too long gone. Her neck is soft, smooth. You end up smooth because each of your moments has rubbed against you. You don't feel it, but it makes you into its evidence. You get worn, everybody does. Being outside wears you faster than anything.

Marilyn whispers and I feel her jaw move, I feel her breathing and her words. I kiss her neck so she won't start to talk about suicide, which I know is coming. I can tell that's the real end of the story, I can taste it in my mouth.

I really need her to be quiet now. Some days suicide pulls itself over your face and your head fills with the dark water and you can't breathe and it wants you. You have to never hear the word.

In the assessment you have to talk about your thinking, every dirty piece. They make you call it down up yourself, the affy darkness, get it waiting for you when you leave their building, the building with no wheelchair access so it's good that you don't need one. You have to talk about your range of movement and show them the limit of what you can do, which means you hurt yourself. They want that, just like Billy. I can't reach or twist the way a person should, not any more, so everything is hard and complicated: the cleaning, the cooking, the washing, the toilet, the whole of what keeps you a person all being taken, all being burned away when you panic, when you're having a bad day.

I had to tell them how sex was and how rape was and what was damaged. The doctors send notes, but the assessment makes me say it and remember and be disgusting. I had to tell them about how love can't happen now. They want everything. Then they tell you that you're well and fit for work. They throw you away with nothing and say you're fit for work and they don't understand how much you want them to be right.

Marilyn is breathing really quickly and it's racing into me.

She disnae mean it. I lift ma heid because I cannae keep it in the one position, no for long.

I can't keep with her this long and she makes this noise when I lift my head away, this wee, small noise, like a child, like a wean that's lonely.

Onetwothreefourfivesixonetwothreefourfivesixsixsixfive fivefivesixsixsix

onetwothreefourfivesix.

When there's naething else, I count the seconds.

Onetwothreefourfivesixonetwothreefourfivesixonetwo threefourfivesix.

One at a time, there they go, the seconds.

Marilyn sways close and she kisses my cheek and her face is wet, her lips are wet and it isn't really me she's kissing. It's a nice lie.

My assessment said I experience only manageable pain.

That was such a nice lie.

Marilyn sighs and leans back against the wall. She's stopped crying, looks younger, cleaned. It's like she's climbed a hard mountain and beat it. I'd cry if it did that to me.

I'd like to tell her that she's beautiful and would have been a beautiful mum. That would let her know she picked the right person to speak to, but I'm still under the water with no light.

Billy's here in the dark. Everyone told me about him, but I married him anyway. He married me. I was stupid in the way he wanted.

I wonder about Marilyn and her husband. I want him to be nice, or to have been nice.

I hear that my mouth is working again and say that I'm sorry, so sorry.

I really want her to be cheerful again. We were talking about which programmes we like on Radio 4. We were being all normal and cosy. Even when someone came, a Tube person in the uniform, he came and asked us to move along, you said you were feeling poorly and that I was looking after you and not to worry.

Such a good lie and he believed her. Marilyn made the Tube person go away.

She starts squeezing my hand and her breathing is jumpy. The sound of it is aching the top of my head and my skin's getting scared of what will happen next. That's because she sounds the way I've sounded. After the grief, that's when Billy would start. You'd taste blood.

There was this rank smell when he made my nose bleed, as if I was rotting, this hot, metal smell of being meat. It would last a few days after.

My mum would have been so ashamed that I let him.

Onetwothreefourfivesixonetwothreefourfivesixonetwo threefourfivesix.

I'm with Marilyn. I think I love her. She was firm with the Tube man, as if she was his gran. She made him embarrassed about himself, made him ask if we were sure that we didn't need help. She just waved her camping trip water bottle at him and said she would take a few sips and be fine. Then he left us. His face looked surprised about what he was doing.

I had to make sure I didn't laugh.

Onetwothreefourfivesixonetwothreefourfivesixonetwo threefourfivesix.

Billy's face just before he got angry was covered in laughter, greasy in smiles.

He smiled when he was happy, too, and I wanted to be glad when he was happy and to be happy with him. But you never could tell.

I wasn't prepared. I had no experience.

Mum made my dad happy and he did that back. Billy kept me away. I didn't know when she was ill, when he was ill. I was no help to them.

It took me too long to get away.

And they gave me a lovely childhood. I had a lovely childhood. I did. I really did.

You've got no chance after that. You have no idea what's coming.

Marilyn has a pack of tissues in her bag and we take one each.

I'm saying to her that Billy didnae do this, he didn't do this part. I was in a women's place after him – me and all these other battered cases. After that I was okay. I was kind of okay and going along and getting better. I had things in place and then they reassessed me.

She gives me another tissue.

Women have tissues because they're something you can give. You see a mess or a sadness and you have something you can give.

Onetwothreefourfivesixonetwothreefourfivesixonetwo threefourfivesix.

And I can see she is just about to really understand me and help me get something worked out and be like a friend, only the Tube man is standing here again and he has these two police.

A lady police and man police.

They're very polite. You know when they do that you're going to be moved on and that the gentleness is there because they feel bad they can do fuck all to help you. And they're nice when there are witnesses – which is Marilyn, she's my witness.

We were sitting in our right place, we were comfortable and friendly. They've spoiled it. Marilyn's getting upset, a fierce kind of upset.

I know she would never have taken me home with her, but I wanted to bide here and think she might. We could have stayed here, stayed for hours and hours.

We weren't doing any harm.

She's being angry for me and it makes me greet.

Onetwothreefourfivesixonetwothreefourfivesixonetwo threefourfivesix.

She is shouting and making her accent sound as if they ought to listen.

Onetwothreefourfivesixonetwothreefourfivesixonetwo threefourfivesix.

Bastards are walking by and smiling as if she's crazy.

Onetwothreefourfivesixonetwothreefourfivesixonetwo threefourfivesix.

I stand up, because when the police lean in and in and tower in over me, it means I'll drown.

The polis don't know I'd made a nice flat for myself alone, clean and bright walls and only a bit of black mould in the high corners of the bathroom and I treated it with bleach. I was quiet and I took in parcels when people were out and I looked after dogs. I was a good neighbour and people were sorry so sorry to see me go.

Onetwothreefourfivesixonetwothreefourfourfourfourfour fourfour.

The standing makes my legs shake.

Onetwothreefourfivesixonetwothreefourfivesixonetwo threefourfivesix.

They want you in the wilderness and out you go.

Onetwothreefourfivesixonetwothreefourfivesixtwotwo twothreefourfive sixfivefourthreetwotwotwotwo.

I want to hug her, but I think I'll fall and we're inside too much of a rush and maybe touching her would make the police angry and she might cling on and I might want that.

I am crying at Marilyn onetwothreefourfivesixoneone oneoneoneoneone onetwothreefourfivesixonetwothreefour fivesix and she is crying at me fourfourfourfourfour and we are trying to be brave.

onetwothreefourfivesixonetwothreefourfivesixonetwo threefourfivesix onetwothreefourfivesixonetwothreefourfive sixtwotwotwothreefourfivesixfivefour threetwotwotwotwo

She smelled of her own clean warm wash onetwothree- fourfivesix and of a perfume I couldn't know.

onetwothreefourfivesixonetwothreefourfivesixtwotwo
twothreefourfive sixfivefourthreetwoonetwothreefourfive
sixonetwothreefourfivesix

She reaches and grabs my arms for this affy, affy while
onetwothreefourfivesix, and then I back away and she has
to let go.

Marilyn onetwothreefourfivesixMarilynonetwothree
fourfivesix

Then she stands and looks at me. She keeps looking at
me but she's shouting at them. Onetwothreefourfivesix.

Onetwothreefourfivesix. This is going to be the last way
I see her, standing under the little sign that says Lost Child
Point.

Onetwothreefourfivesix.

Lost Child Point.

Onetwothreefourfivesix.

Like it's geography onetwothreefourfivesix and geography is something you can't change.

Onetwothreefourfivesix.

Harm like it's mountains and nobody can do anything
about mountains.

Marilyn said it was the point for lost children and we
were home.

Onetwothreefourfivesixoneseventwothreefourfivesixone
twothreefourfivesixonetwothreefourfivesixonefourtwothree
fourfivesixonetwothreefourfivesixonetwothreefourfivesixone
twothreefourfivesixfiveonetwothreefourfivesixonetwothree
fourfivesixonetwothreefourfivesixonetwothreefourfivesixone
twosixthreefourMarilynfivesixonetwothreefourfivesixone
twothreefourfivesixonetwothreefourfivesixonetwothreefour

fivesixonetwotwotwotwotwothreefourfivesixMarilynthree
onetwothreefourfivesixonetwothreefourfivesixonetwothree
fourfivesixonetwothreefourfivesixonetwothreefourthreefive
sixonetwo

  Marilyn.

Even Words Have Meaning

They do still kill themselves, of course, but not in the numbers we saw last spring. Our sector seems quite tranquil now, there's only this gently domestic tumble into graves: a few each week. One might say that a series of afterthoughts and pent-up disappointments have been duly expressed by a policeman or administrator here and a family there. The crimes were epidemic and they still continue to produce epidemic results. Permitting your life to be entirely wrong and then having to know it is hard. The realisation is far too large to accommodate and can tear what ought to be whole. It can make any serious chap with a secretive pistol end his last impermissible weaknesses and pains. He may also prefer that his wife and perhaps his children disappear.

Although naturally suicides with guns are scarce these days. We've been rather keen, for obvious reasons, to disarm the population. They are largely compliant. They are, to be frank, desperately compliant. For the most part adults here are as meek as children, smiling with confusion, or fear, or some shameful need that we cannot help them to fulfil. The children move stiffly and look bewildered. Ask decently for anything and most of them think you don't mean it.

The women's faces are soft and like a type of constant pleading. They suggest sad wishes in hiding.

And there is great hiding after great mistakes: uniforms in shallow graves, belt buckles in gardens, incinerated photographs, identity cards, papers. There has been a determination in many households to be newborn again. It's a human desire, really quite a habit apparently, to dig pits and fill them with ashes and assume this will make all well. I've come to believe this shows a cracked way of thinking.

We know there are weapons still out of our hands, some of them drowning in rivers and lakes. Others are sleeping in attics and the dark places made needful by all of the larger darknesses. And it's relatively simple to unwrap the Walther, the Mauser, Sauer, Steyr, Dreyse, Astra – they had so many kinds of pistol – maybe clean your choice, take time before your final firing. They only shoot their loved ones and themselves now, never us. The bullets rarely miss, determination having been so much admired and practised until just lately. It is terrible, I would imagine, to have no one left to obey when screaming and threats were all that made your madhouse feel like home.

Their teeth stay gritted even once their brains are blown. This makes the current dead seem vexed.

We've all of us seen a range of dying. In our circumstances a fellow becomes more than passingly familiar with the broader variations: the terribly large and altered sunshine corpses, the uncanny cold-weather bodies that can't hold you back with a stink and therefore invite too much study. The stiff bodies reach and gesture precisely as they might in life and nonetheless are precisely done with and quite foolish. Such a bad winter in '44: generously freezing.

The weather troubled us as we moved eastward through Belgium, watching for trench foot and then frostbite. We limped and ached. There was mud and water and shattered water, shattered mud, there were trees and men in splinters, and I do have to emphasise that such conditions were not what we'd grown accustomed to withstanding. We'd spent two years and more getting our knees brown on the far side of the Med. We had been careful not to mind the friendly scorpions too much, nor the salt that would stiffen our shirts and the raw skin resulting, nor the sandflies. Then we didn't mind the ghibli blowing in and blinding us, platoon after platoon. We choked now and then and we grumbled about some silly bastard blitzing hell and knocking it all into powder and onto us. Inconsiderate. One doesn't imagine that so much dust is in amongst the sand, ready to fly. The thirst that it gives you is vicious and intimate, like nothing else, except perhaps the loss of hope, the loss of love. They're both much the same thing, really.

We first made ourselves friends with cursing at the dust. I was an oddity arriving kitted out like a Mayfair captain, fresh from Gieves & Hawkes, but sporting inexplicable green epaulettes. The men came up slowly, as horses or dogs with sad histories might, testing their trust. One must be quiet around long-fighting men, there should be no speaking unless required, no line-shooting, no bravura. People are simple as beasts under pressure: they need peace and I tried to provide it. One may be a War Correspondent, but one has to offer peace. That was my guess and I was lucky.

Every one of us looked for luck. Men under such conditions always do.

And meanwhile the desert drew us out thin across its miles and miles. It stretched the mind. I had been a man of hedgerows, Cotswold stone and Portland stone and London brick, haycocks and rivers, not this shouting light, this murdering sort of beauty, the charge in the openness. We all had been more civilised in other times and other places, but we had been smaller, too. The desert grows you. Before we met it, we hadn't walked as easily, or stood in the ways men do when they are becoming absolute.

We were soldiers: even I was a kind of soldier: but our uniforms and attitudes were highly deregulated. We recomposed ourselves for our hardships and to suit our circumstances: corduroys and suede boots with a soft sole, pullovers and sheepskins for the nights. We exercised our flights of fancy in funny headgear. We felt we were close beneath God's eye and needn't attend to more minor authorities. We invented strange prayers and our souls grew complicated, although we started out as the standard-issue type of men from standard-issue places.

Parker was from Lancashire, Mayburg was Hull. Silvers was from Liverpool, or near there. The two MacNeills were both Argyll, but not related, not brothers. I say that although all of us were, as we put it, brothers in sand. Williams was London and Farrelly was too. Or so they said. We could have been anyone, to be truthful. The desert founds religions, boils up laws and fundamentals out of mountains and wide nights. Except for Stillwell we were nothing it couldn't alter.

Stillwell: he seemed to walk out and meet the desert like a childhood pal and be glad. He wasn't from any location we could imagine. Stillwell was born wherever you found him, himself for the duration. The desert loved him and he loved it back. They were mutually admiring.

There were other chaps, ones who came later, replacements replacing replacements, but I don't recall them, or their names.

One grows tired of knowing people who won't last.

I find it, these days, very difficult to know things, or remember. I flinch when a door slams and my head feels broken. This isn't unusual, but also isn't right.

One had imagined the future as something very clear and had assumed that, once our war was over, a fresh green time would spring up and invite us. We kept busy, wanting to burrow out all of the death and the bringers of death and the wrongs, the wrongness. We died filthily to end the filthiness, or else avoided dying and lived on filthily. Yet those replaced and those replacing did mostly intend to go home and be free.

We had this type of expectation that kept us moving, kept us fighting, but now we are stilled and our war is over, we can see that our hope was nonsense. Cynicism colours every breath. This is, in part, because the attitude of armies, the infantry mindset, is always betrayed: enduring but disappointed. This is also, in part, because the nature of our species gives no cause for optimism. We've seen too much of it. I don't say so, I don't write this for any publication, there being no way to describe it and no readers susceptible to understanding.

My eyes make my position clear. People avoid them.

My face is no longer pleasant. I have to admit I catch glimpses of it reflected while the neat local barber does his work. I find myself sickening and make his hand tremble.

And I've realised, as we all have, that nowhere will be free for us in the way the desert was. We also are sure that the filthiness isn't done with: it has tucked itself into nice places and is digging in. No one who matters, it seems, can have faith in effective leaders who are also kind and not even a little bit covered in filth. They let Badoglio run Italy: a leader who happily served under Mussolini. Franco will stay in Spain, as if he wasn't a Fascist dictator and isn't still a Fascist dictator and didn't beg his power from two other Fascist dictators. They're all of them clowns, those types, and somewhere they know it and it makes them twist in peculiar ways: they get to be clowns who like torture. They need the blood and worship to make them believe they are serious and secure. They think a beaten face won't laugh at them.

A chap up from Naples told me that Victor Emmanuel, the midget would-be king, had himself chauffeured from his hideout in Vietri down to a farm in Paestum, nearly forty miles and never mind the petrol, because there he could buy eggs two lire cheaper than at home. Flunkeys, arranged in order of rank, formed up between the farmhouse and his Fiat limousine, passing the eggs one by one to the Foreign Office favourite for Italy's future. He held each egg up to the light like a wary housewife, before he would set it down in his royal basket. Greedy, thin-skinned and stupid: anyone could buy such a tiny man. That's why he's the FO's idea of a born leader.

Too many of us now have seen real leaders: ones who led, who saved us, who were kind. Going home, we will expect nobility and mercy and be disappointed.

No, that's not right. Going home, we will mourn nobility and mercy. We won't expect them, but they will be missed. The government of the country for which I have been fighting wants Italy to be a docile monarchy again. This is because, not so long ago, Milan was full of ordinary people, absolutely, wonderfully still alive and processing across the Piazza Loreto. When they reached the petrol station they paused for a while and looked up at the iron-work portico that covered the petrol pumps. That's where the Communists and Socialists had hung up la Petacci, Mussolini's girl, and half a dozen of his PNF *gherarchis* and fat Mussolini himself.

Il Duce Ha Sempre Ragione. No one but a clown would insist he was always right, have it plastered on every patriotic wall.

And there he was, as dead as corpses get, still dressed in a T-shirt and riding britches and German high-topped boots, a part of the disguise he'd tried to run away in. His Majesty's Government, with its love of overblown cowards and fear of Reds, swiftly found the whole affair perturbing.

It was such an occurrence: a day when humiliation and power were inappropriately allocated: the one in the place of the other. Yes, perturbing.

The chap up from Naples, another Correspondent, described the scene for his readers at home. He told them it was chaotic: an animalistic and foreign chaos. Nothing else would have been acceptable to the censors. But he told me the square was silent, apart from the soft fall of so many footsteps. No one spoke, or tried to touch the hanging bodies, which were guarded by the Reds. Sometimes a figure would pause and nod to themselves, as if they were once again able to look at reality, see it and concur. Then they would walk on, slowly, gently.

Really almost anyone might end up walking slowly, gently, implacably past a failed leader, a destroyer finally destroyed, and the FO knows it, all our remaining governments know it. Fear of us is hiding in amongst them like dust amongst sand. They can feel it choke them.

In the desert, my brothers and I understood that our superiors did not care too much for us and were not, in many ways, superior. We sometimes would feel we were being used as a sadly necessary strength, but sometimes we felt we'd turned into an unloved idea they were intent on changing. Sometimes we were a way of proving theories and sometimes what happened to us was somebody else's mistake. No one said sorry. No one ever does. Our losses were inevitable. We were there to be lost until our enemy had lost more. The Tommy is there, will always be there, to obey and be resolute. I was there to report on his constant resolution. I was there to suggest that we served a purpose, that the living would one day be honoured along with the dead.

My father was a Tommy once himself. Now he spends his days flinching and lying down in his study. Nights are for screaming. Whoever he was when my mother loved him has been mislaid. She wrote to say the bombing raids made him peaceful, could I perhaps bring back some Mills bombs.

But Tommies must never, ever bring their wars back home.

I always have resembled my father in photographs.

I write to her about wild flowers, there are alpines here. And I write to the readers of Britain that Germans have given obedience a bad name. I have been careful to praise obedience in itself. I do not question the beautiful truths in a chain of command. My duty lies in making everyone aware, once more, that foreign chaps command extremely badly, don't take to it and cannot be bred for it. When the British command, wherever we command, we must assume it never does us any harm. Our colonies must also, in peacetime, become docile and happy to be led. Colonies must never, ever take the war back home. I have come to believe this shows a cracked way of thinking.

I want to send words back home. They're what I have, they should be what I have. I want to be clear, I want to eradicate dust, I want to send whole messages back to my own country, ones that will let it be my own country, keep it as a home for me. The sentences jumble, though. I can hardly type, can't write a letter, can't sign my name. I have unreliable hands. Whatever I say leaves a copper kind of taste behind it. I am not a Good Correspondent.

I waste paper. I am a Squander Bug. But I can get more.

There's a fellow in town who supplies me – calls himself Professor Heine. His university fired him in '38, apparently, because Germany's clowns disliked most forms of learning, beyond those required for the proper use and maintenance of weapons, or the inculcation of consoling and minatory phrases. He had a hard time, but as a sign of hope returning, he has resurrected his old title. He deals mainly in black-market cigarettes and penicillin, but has a sideline in textbooks, pen nibs, paper, ink, and has retained an educational bearing. I talk to him over the real American coffee he brings with him. This isn't fraternising. I am finding out information. I am looking for words. I no longer need friends and he has no wish to be one. This suits us both.

The professor had a fondness for the Berlin Philharmonic which, given the circumstances, has a recent history that is predictably sad. One conductor fled to Switzerland before the Gestapo could get him. His replacement was shot last August. There was a misunderstanding at a checkpoint. British driver, American sentry: things were bound to go wrong. The conductor chap was guiltless, remarkably for the time, had even been involved with some kind of resistance. Still, even after it was over, the war killed him. That's the thing about a war nobody mentions – the tragedies and terrible accidents and losses that come from it won't stop until the very last person who touched it, breathed it, saw it, tasted it, until the last person who knew it, or who was harmed by the filthiness of it is gone, a corpse and gone and done for.

Heine told me the Philharmonic's final concert during the rule of the clowns was rounded off by the arrival of polite and only mildly threatening Hitlerjugend doling out cyanide capsules to the whole of the audience.

If clowns believe they're done for, they can't believe anyone else could live without them. And they don't believe anyone should. Cyanide for enemies, cyanide for friends. If history here was music, cyanide would be the leitmotif.

Leitmotiv.

German word.

Guiding motive.

Leitprinzip.

Guiding principle.

Useful.

Anyone can have any words, though, can't they? The trouble is, you have to mean them. And you have to go on meaning them. If you don't, they're simply noises: no meaning at all.

I wrote last week about the authorities who are now vetting conductors – asking who stayed, who ran, who did a bit of both and why. Assessment of guilt is ongoing, if imperfect.

When my sand brothers and I laughed at blackened limbs in a burned-out tank, or picked a corpse's pocket, stole its boots, when we shot the dead to make them deader and stop their staring and when I had to do filthy things in order to live, to blink, to swallow, to eat, feel heartbeats, scream, live, just to live: these were not things to be glad of. And maybe Rommel was a gentleman and didn't like Hitler too much, but he still killed a lot of us. There were a number of early good choices he didn't make. Perhaps he confused obedience with honour.

Kein Leitprinzip.

I hear the thinking of our enemies go echoing about when I want silence. It's in the dust and brickwork, it's going home in our packs. Everything in the world that's clean is still getting dusty, still in the storm, and I can't exactly see. I wake every morning breathless and I think of Stillwell. I remember him. When I die, I am perfectly sure that Stillwell will be there.

Stillwell was with us in the dunes and flats, the desert scrubland. Together we were all of us drunk on the space that invited us to roar across it. We experienced war without impediment and served as we could whenever our commanders and our enemies saw fit. Both shared a tendency to harm us. We rarely bore a grudge. We believed that we were necessary and that we were doing right. We trusted those ideas which have proved fragile, or incompatible with the time.

Later, after Stillwell, we were sent up to the northern forests and the treachery of dips and rises, endless nights of mutilation, wet greenery and man burrows. We really didn't quite take to the Ardennes. Stillwell wasn't with us, couldn't guide us and that made it worse.

And, in the end, our orders have brought me all the way to here – to these despicably lovely mountains and houses that are too old not to be rotten and these thin and crooked streets, pretty bay windows and painted walls, painted with saints, blind and useless saints. The buildings lean in towards each other across the lanes and put you in shadows perpetually. The war never reached here, not so you can see. It thought the thoughts, but tried to duck the damage.

We hate it. I hate it. I should be accurate.

And I have no more jokes to make it better.

Back in our beginning, our young dog days, long before we'd even reached the Derna–Mechili track, I became known for comedy patter. There was no other use for cleverness at that time and I am a Cambridge man; I am provably clever. Even Cockney Farrelly didn't make them entertained the way I could.

We were twice in Mersa Matruh. I said it sounded medical, or like a curse. Not much of a joke to start with, but it was something and we laughed together, my brothers and then myself. We were happy, barking out wild noises in the way that fighting taught us to loosen our fear, or light up a wait.

I have never laughed the way I did up until the surrender. None of us have. We never will. Without our war, nothing is funny.

The big golden letter C on my cap – we decided that declared me Comic not Correspondent. And my brothers would come to me, more often in the beastly times than not, and I would be their fool. I was funny in numerous, at the time, undisclosed locations: Sidi Barrani and Beda Fomm, Tobruk, Medenine. I am late of Jesus College and Medenine.

Stillwell went away from us at Medenine. Somehow, they took him. We can't say he was lost. He was never known to be lost. He was the finest and wisest of desert men, born with a capacity to understand parched directions. Stillwell could follow the curve and hollow of nothing at all, a blank heaving with heat, and bring us home. Twice we would have died, but he walked us back. He could taste light from the North, could Stillwell. As soon as he'd stepped ashore at Sollum the reports were that he'd fainted, dropped. Then he woke up in a guardhouse on a stretcher and knew himself different, ready, all awake. From then on he had the ways. He understood everything: the sunfalls, the delicate lie of surfaces over mines, the scents of safety, old trails, wadis, petrol dumps, the route to Medenine.

Medenine.

It didn't sound like anything to us.

We were used, by then, to keeping watch in wasteland nights – the cold and the stars like splinters of phosphorous poking through. At Medenine there was fog and it turned every one of us homesick, homesoft and discontented. It wasn't fair. It must have thrown Stillwell off.

We didn't see him dead, not at once. And it is good that he never became just one of the corpses in our minds: those strangers with puzzled eyes, sunk eyes, out eyes, the mummy limbs gone drifting into sand, the wet splitting, the unlikely and missing faces, the burned who are brittle and twist. He wasn't burned. We were glad of that, when we knew it.

Nobody speaks about him. His name became something we didn't have to mention, always there among us, quiet between the words. And I never have written about Stillwell, because he was our man, our brother and a personal matter. But those of us who knew him are diminished. There's only me.

I want him to last, but I can't mention Stillwell to the new chaps: they wouldn't understand.

I am accustomed to all of the words and the people that I don't mention and can't mention. I have never disclosed positions or operational details. I'm not a traitor. And it was made clear that I need not write articles naming our losses, agonies, howling, or the numbers of the dead. The enemy's corpses should not be dwelt upon and ours must hardly exist. Our deaths must be full of urgent nobility. The jolly Tommy is a vision of delighted sacrifice. He disappears into an undefined but orderly cessation which will cause no distress to his relatives and loved ones. No Tommy calls for his mother. No Tommy screams like an animal and loses himself in blood. Or if he does I have never told the reader so.

And only the other side shat in their own foxholes under fire.

And no publication would print how we loved Stillwell and were never the same.

The dead can stare at me – they do stare and no one can shoot them any more – but none of them have been my fault, not exactly. I never kill, I only write. The brothers fought and I sent my descriptions of how they were not in vain, of how there was an air drop once, a jovially quixotic solo flight curving over us and back and letting loose a mildly miraculous canister of magazines, tinned ham and almost unbroken whisky. After the usual checks for booby traps we accepted it as a good thought from our generous blue god: the one who understands us and bends near under strafing and within the detonations of H.E.

Now there are no more explosions our God is too far away.

And somewhere in a country I believe no longer exists my Ministry of Information continues to read the words that I have left. I continue to build morale and faith in the promise of the British Way and Purpose. The dreams of continuing mass education, unified effort, reward of merit and protection of the weak will prevent returning soldiers from keeping their weapons and associated skills. Everyone is rather keen, for obvious reasons, to disarm the population. Men and women will return, containing the memory of a space in which they could be always absolute, complete. They will be discontented.

But slowly their dreams will be changed. Dreams are only dust, they blow about.

Aus der Traum.

Being deceived and then having to know it is hard. We will find it hard.

Naturally, I don't write about that.

This afternoon I will file a piece about a study with a Chinese rug, a little blood on it, redpurple sticky in a patch where one of the local doctors rested his head. He hit himself near the temple on the corner of his desk as he fell. That didn't kill him. Dr Doktor Taschner had bitten a proper old Tesch & Stabnow Zyankalikapsel – a glass phial of cyanide. They're rather rare now, most of those who owned one having availed themselves already.

Taschner hadn't done anything much according to the standards of the time. He had simply doled out *Gnadentode – mercy deaths*. Mercy was highly popular here, even before what we might call the outbreak of hostilities. The doctor had skimmed through reports and put little plus signs on forms and sent them off and that was very easy to do and he'd hardly have felt that later and somewhere else too many plus signs totalled up would send your relative with the bad nerves, or that chap with the uncomplicated mind, or you with your spastic limbs into a gas van, or a killing room.

Mountains of the dead, achieved with remarkable ease – the kind of smooth operation bound to encourage larger murders and overreaching. The pits, the ashes, the glittering piles of spectacles, the stacked-up suitcases packed with intended futures and all of those objects that hoped to ward off foreseeable suffering and distresses contained within in a sane world. Mercy summoned up the machinery for that.

I organised a ride to one of the liberated KLs: empty huts, empty scaffolds, empty watchtowers. But the pits very full of ashes. Afterwards, I burned my clothes. It was impossible to get the stink out – the reek of fear, blood, shit, sweat, piss, burning. There should not ever be such a thing in the world.

I didn't send an article. There is an editorial appetite for the terrible at present. We have done terrible things, but not so terrible as their things, not so terrible as that, the hate running mad and triumphant, burning with human fat. We were only in a war, we were not unstoppably wallowing in bones, in women's hair, in every bad thing we could think of to comfort our unease. We did not consent to act out the fantasies of crippled little clowns and keep on because we were taking Pervitin and never slept, keep on because we were always drunk to do the things one can only do when one had drowned one's heart, keep on because see how terrible we are – what if anyone ever remembers, ever says? They will destroy all. They will make us think and also one does not wish to be murdered for not murdering and one is afraid deeply and only for oneself and now one has sunk this deep one can't admit to the stench of evaporated people and rotting people and terrified people in one's uniform.

They used to play with their children, sing songs, organise film shows.

I do not have the words for telling anybody that.

It is very hard to think of, the mind shies away.

But the new blood always fountains up from underground in summer. The air dies. Dynamite the chimneys, tear down the fences, plant trees – it will still always be there and be screaming.

When I go home I cannot tell anyone, not anything, not my mother, my father, my sister, not touch anyone I love with this. If I start to tell a stranger I will only be able to say that screaming is screaming.

People here have their own small stories, little bits of hell. Old Professor Heine told me first about the phenol injections Herr Doktor Taschner gave to little Katja

Schwering and poor Franz Griezmann. Taschner was of the opinion that the children weren't quite right, not right enough to live. Certainly, he didn't himself go on to kill Jews, or gypsies, or Socialists, or drug addicts, helpless drinkers, homosexuals, or Communists, or Christians who insisted on it, Slavs, or any of the almost everyone who eventually wasn't quite right. The doctor only killed two children. And he made sure that elsewhere other people would meet his few troubling cases, barely a hundred, and kill them. Burdens on the state every one of them who might not have lived that long, maybe only another ten or twenty years. And perhaps he was of the opinion that they were in pain, or looked inexplicable, infectious, uninvincible. So they deserved the administration of Mercy.

But the two children, yes, he did kill them with his own hands.

The Schwering mother came to see him this Monday. She must have been finally overwhelmed by an impulse. She was carrying with her, as everyone has repeated, her daughter's coat, a bright blue coat which was extremely handsome and expensive and would have looked so becoming on a loved little girl. It was almost new and made one think of Sundays and another decade, not this decade, not the one before.

Mother Schwering had walked up and down the high street, walked through perhaps every street in town, carrying her daughter's coat with her daughter's ghost inside it, and then she stood outside the merciful death doctor's office door. He wouldn't let her in. But the next day he was dead and spoiling that Chinese rug with the doctor's blood and his wife screaming.

The Taschners had no children of their own. I suppose his wife will have nothing left of him beyond any unburned photographs and that stain.

The Schwering mother lost her husband to some Russian prison camp and her sons to graves. She has the coat left and the knowledge that she trusted the wrong doctor. She trusted a number of wrong things. She screams a good deal.

If there had been screaming earlier, if there had been screaming at once, at the first sign of madness, if there were always screaming: I wonder then how we might prosper.

The coat, the mother, the names of the children: these are details that make for a more effective piece.

I saw Taschner dead. He was on a stretcher but uncovered, because it had been decided that no one liked him and he need have no dignity. I will mention his grey stubble, his greyed shirt collar that was showing wear.

Taschner gave me the customary clifftop feeling I get from every corpse: as if I might be standing, having stepped out away from a cliff, as if I were hanging in high air. I feel that the world is about to take note of me harshly, about to apply the customary laws and make me drop. I don't scream when I see them. Perhaps I should and this would make them peaceful, like my father with his happy bombs.

Stillwell I never saw dead – we didn't, I didn't, couldn't. When we searched in the morning there was a black and greasy crater, the smell of pork and ash and sulphur. There was a boot we recognised as his. We didn't look in it.

A week later, Farrelly dreamed that Stillwell walked up and found him, Stillwell limping with a bloodied foot. Stillwell shook his hand. And by the afternoon Farrelly had caught one, a nasty stomach wound, his hand paddling in the blood while Parker tried to get a field dressing on him, disinfecting powder and all that. Farrelly lasted until night-fall – we couldn't get him out, not just then, and that was unlucky for him.

Farrelly called out Stillwell's name, as if he saw him coming and was glad.

That started us thinking. Maybe Stillwell came for Farrelly. And maybe he would keep on leading us out and bringing us safe, bringing us to a safe home. We didn't want to die, but if we had to, we needed a friend to be there with us.

I understand that we were superstitious. We were afraid. We collected souvenirs without knowing why. The boots and wristwatches we took made sense – one does need them – and Lugers are something one might sell or keep. A picture of a stranger's children, small things out of cold pockets, burned toys out of buildings: there was no reason for them. We stole as if we were walking altars and needed offerings. When the clutter got too heavy, we'd announce the fact and throw bits of it away.

I wasn't the only one who knew that we dropped the treasures for Stillwell to see as he followed us, perhaps for Stillwell to pick up.

He did follow, was following.

Williams, Mayburg, Silvers: every one of them called out to Stillwell as they went. They saw him.

There's just me now, the Bad Correspondent. Only one left.

I would like to stay here and be well again and able to think and then I'd write. I would make words that were better than screaming and then I would go back to my hedgerows and haycocks and they would be clean, the world would be clean, and I'd sit in a chair in my father's study and he would read and I would write as if I believed that even words have meaning. I would keep on.

But I don't know if Stillwell could find me over there.

He's out amongst the people in the town here, I can feel him. He's waiting for me behind all these averagely filthy people who did the average human thing and decided their safety was more important than anything, than screaming. They did their best. People do their best. It isn't very good. The fear tends to change them.

That's why we invented pistols, I suppose.

And people hide their pistols, because of the guilt. And people have to search for the pistols, because of the danger.

There are so many weapons about the place it's hard to keep track.

The pistol I took is resting at the bottom of my pack, wrapped in a shirt. I wasn't supposed to be armed in wartime, but in peace I have a gun.

Stillwell already knows that. In the same way he knows I will call for him when it's time.

After the bullet, just in that moment when nothing is quite done with, I believe I will see him and call and reach out. He will take my hand.

I'm not afraid. One has to be anything other than afraid. That is important.

New Mexico

Hi, my name is Phoebe Delray and this is *PTP* and here we go again.

And would you believe it? This is Episode 100 of our motherlovin' *Post Traumatic Podcast*. The *PTP*. We made it. And because this is a special occasion I have no guest. Usually, we like a variety of voices and perspectives on the old cases and the cold cases and the issues we look at. And I personally love our forensic and legal deep dives. I love our forensic guests and I know you do, too. And our legal guests.

None of our guests are *illegal*. Because *No Person Is Illegal*. And that I have to point this out fries my brain. We truly live in horrible, horrible times. But then, we always kinda have and sometimes it hits one type of people and sometimes it hits another. Which is partly why we have this show – for the people who get hit more often than not.

Anyway – I have no guest this episode and I will eventually tell you why.

There will be an explanation, but first I am so sorry for the goddam noise. I thought I'd come back to my home studio here, where I started out, to record our hundredth episode. Some of you listening were with me way back then and thank you for sticking around. If you scroll down on the site, you can find the early pods and the early, I think we can say, basic sound quality. Enjoy that on your walk-around, waterproof Bluetooth speakers. And right now – as you can hear – we are having just the most Colorado type of Colorado hailstorm. Crazy hailstones pretty much the size of softballs are happening right now. This is what we get out here – the big weather, the mountain weather. And, of course, we have the wolves and wolverines and bears – and those yellow-bellied marmots.

Sure, they never did a wrong deed to anyone, those marmots, but you can see in their eyes that if they were bigger they would try. They are not yellow-bellied, they are waiting to evolve and grow.

It's a little bit of a Death Paradise out here with the storms and the snows and the animals – including the small, resentful marmots – and that's before you add the people. As we know, the greatest and most dangerous and prolific and imaginative predators on earth would be *the people*.

Thanks, though, on this special occasion to all of you amazing, non-predator people who are not monsters in human clothing and who've got me through this far. Thanks for your messages, as ever, and for signing up to support what I do and therefore paying for the cool website and the snazzy editing and technical stuff from Loretta the genius, there has to be one Loretta on every high-quality podcast. She's here, too – up in the thin Colorado air.

Hello, as well, to all of you who showed up at the live gig in Brooklyn last week. We had such a blast. Also thank you for the sugar skulls. So many of you are my sugar mommas and sugar daddies and we love those sugar skulls, even just because they are an expression of care and solidarity. Never mind that they let you eat death and crap it right back out again, or that it celebrates and warms the cold certainty of the grave and all of that. We got – lordy – about forty-eight Brooklyn skulls, I think. Which is enough to put Loretta and me in some kinda coma, so some of them also went to other good places and people. Great to know so many people get my *Día de los Muertos* obsessions.

Gonna get me a new *calaveritas de azúcar* tattoo on the other arm this very week, in fact – a skull with the marigolds under the chin and a desert bluebell in each eye. Those are blue, blue, just the bluest Mohave flowers if you have not come across them. They spring up after rains in the desert and I would say they make the land the sky.

That's the plan for this week after we wrap the show – I'll be getting my fifth tattoo. Turning pain into beauty, because we can. It will be on a significant date and it will also celebrate this hundredth instalment of fun. I'll have a big day of ink and then come down off that endorphin high, chill a little and then get the research done for next week which will be a stellar week for you – many, many great guests. I'll post photos of the latest skull as soon as it's all healed.

And finally, before we really, really get going, I have to recommend the great products of On Your Road Security. On Your Road make stylish but sturdy bags designed specifically for the female traveller. That means everything fits your body and your spine and the straps aren't catering only to the six-foot jarhead kind of human on the move. The military have travel gear of their own, goddammit. Some of us are dainty and we want our shit to stay safe, right? That's why On Your Road provide slash-proof pockets, tamper-proof locks and extendable cables for those locks so you can lasso your bag to a table or a bench, or a six-foot jarhead, or such. There's a full range of colours and designs and most have a convenient solar panel recharger gizmo which has rescued me muchly when I have a script to write, or research to do and I'm out of juice, on the move and there are no power points. Yes, I stay in the classier hotels now, but that was not always the case and On Your Road is great for your less tech-friendly accommodation options and for those long bus rides and whatnot. When your motel host is over-fond of stuffed animals and looks at you and asks *What's a Internet?* – you have On Your Road.

I mostly use the Amagordo Travel Purse and the Sioux Falls Carry-on. That's a combination which makes sense of all my weird talismanic shit and squares it away. I can find things in the many sane and adjustable storage areas. None of the bags ever has to have a black interior that instantly loses your crap in some kind of existential outer space shadowland. I picked the interior colour – there's a whole colour chart you can select from – and I chose Colcothar of Vitriol, because that is a real colour, not an elf king or a walk-on nude in *Game of Thrones*. The colours available are popping and wonderful and the attention to design, detail and construction lets me know that On Your Road are people like us: obsessive-compulsive paranoiacs who are putting that energy to positive use.

And we need to stay personally safe on our road. So every luggage item has an easy-to-reach alarm which is loud as hell. Most bags include a high-power torch you can either use to guide down a landing aircraft and find lost contact lenses in neighbouring states, or to blind an attacker. Some also feature a highly accessible harmless, aircraft-safe, colour-dye spray – if you want to tag that asshole who just tried something – or a pepper spray if that's legal where you are. Your stuff will be safe, you will be safe, you will look like a superhero enjoying her well-earned downtime. And if you're a gentleman of more slender build, you can be safe, too. What else can I say? I'd be endorsing this, even if they didn't pay me to, but they do, which is cool. You too can live this life – be given free shit and paid to enjoy it.

Believe in yourself, be true to that, follow your joy – and wait a whole bunch of years until you've pretty much given up on the world as a merciful place. That's when it all works out. Resist those impulses to self-harm, just so you can own your torment, hang on tight and then the free stuff and fun starts happening.

We paid in advance, though, right? We paid in advance.

Anyhoo, back to *PTP*. Last week, we looked at some of the Ted Bundy survivors, like Kathy Kleiner who was attacked in Chi Omega House at Florida State where she had every reason to expect she would be secure, able to sleep and wake up unharmed. After the attacks, she was found rocking back and forth, face covered in blood, some of her teeth in the bedclothes, jaw broken – just rocking and managing to ask for her boyfriend of the time and her pastor, which is heartbreaking. She was just a sweet young woman assaulted murderously in her sleep by a coward. There in the same room was Karen Chandler. She was also horribly beaten with a wooden branch by a monster who doesn't get to be called handsome, or intelligent. Bundy the killer's current public status as smart and cute just means that he gamed the media, like he tried to game law enforcement, the legal system and the wider world in his pursuit of opportunities to kill women and to rape them, before and after that. He groomed the media, he made himself what they wanted him to be: this big mystery – *Oh, how come an 'attractive' guy is a maniac?*

Look at his eyes. Look at his hole-in-ground empty eyes. Look at that secret smile he gets, which normal people misunderstand. In a standard-issue human being that kind of smile is flirtatious. That smile is about sharing a secret with one other person, probably something sexual. It's the expression of a person you either already know, or will enjoy knowing, because they're trying to guess what you might like – that's the secret. They're trying to understand you and the secrets of what you'll both like.

That's not what Bundy's smile is about. Bundy is redefining you and you don't know it – that's the secret, it's all his secret. He is smiling because he knows that he can kill you at any time, that he can turn you into a screaming puppet, or a decapitated body that he can have sex with, or whatever else occurs to him, whatever he has time for. His secret is that you're wrong when you assume you have a right to live, or to expect that civilisation will exist everywhere you go. His secret is your being alive isn't permanent, that your identity doesn't matter. That's not flirtatious. That's demonic. And every time he flashed his grin the media lapped it up, the shutters clicked, the cameras rolled, even though it was an insult to everyone alive, especially women.

He gets that smile when he's able to put his traumatised victims on the stand and just stroke his way back through the crimes, or when he makes a cop describe every detail of the crime scenes, the wreckage Bundy made. He longed for everyone to itemise those super-sweet details of horror and dominance for him. He's a creep and a predator who didn't get into a good school, or get great qualifications – he was no genius. He had one purpose – being a horror machine that killed women. He was good at satisfying his own perverse needs, because that was all he ever thought about, all that mattered. He wasn't distracted by saving someone pain, or loving someone, or understanding anyone other than himself as anything other than a mark.

Broadcasters, even back then, would rather give screen time to a narcissist freak than – *oh my God, no* – *this would shock people* – give the appalling details of crimes which would show him for the monster he is. He's the kind of man who would bite off a young woman's nipple, let's just say that. He's a man who would kill a twelve-year-old girl – Kimberly Leach. Remember her name. Forget his. That's shocking, it's supposed to be shocking. Finding that shocking keeps us all safe.

I know I talk about this a lot, but we have this horrendous situation where everyone knows fucking Bundy's name, but not the names of his victims, those poor sweet slaughtered women that he tortured and mutilated, because he was a rage-filled asshole tormented by his grandiosity while it fought with his many immensely obvious inadequacies.

And he was a Republican Party campaigner. Of course. Psychopaths always advocate for political systems they hope will let them hunt and feed at will. And feel free to buy my book *What To Do When Narcissist A**holes Take Over Your Country* – it is now available at all good bookstores and online from the website. It's a wonderful Thanksgiving gift. You can send a copy to all those relatives you can no longer talk to over Thanksgiving, because a black man was elected president in 2008 and their penises have not grown back to full size ever since, so now they can't stop yelling about how they are being replaced.

Thanksgivings are tricky, yeah? For many reasons.

Or you can just buy the book for your personal reading pleasure.

Some of us have families we were born with and can give thanks for and some of us make families of choice. We can all make a place of love and eat pumpkin pie in safety together with those we love, whenever we like, not just on an anniversary of colonial genocide and turkey murder. So there's that.

My family is not a problem at Thanksgiving. It's not around, as some of you will know. That's a different problem, no longer having a birth family, but I have my family of choice. And I have my tattoos and my ass-kicking life.

Just to finish last week's rant – I didn't get to mention the wonderful Carol Daronch, who was an eighteen-year-old high school graduate when Bundy tried to abduct her. She stayed alert and even though she did get in the car with him – we always say *never get in the car* – she kept thinking and noticing as he was lying and lying to her, driving along on his way to murder her. Even when he'd managed to put one handcuff on her and pulled out a gun, she resisted. She jumped out of his car and fought for her life while he hit her with a tyre iron. And she talks about him having these 'beady, blank, lifeless eyes' which does not sound attractive or functional or handsome to me. It does sound like accurate observation. Carol Daronch is a survivor, she escaped with her life and her testimony led the police to Bundy's shitty little Volkswagen and led to his first arrest.

Four hours after Carol escaped, Bundy killed Debra Kent, because that was his purpose for the day – find a woman, kill a woman.

And these days we know more and we're more alert and we can listen to podcasts and try to keep each other safe here with information. Carol was alert and observant and courageous. That's all very well if you're awake. Those poor girls at Florida State University – and bear in mind the survivors of that attack were not given the support they needed – those young women just went to sleep in their beds at night, like you should be able to. We need to be able to go to sleep, ladies, and still stay safe.

That's what I'm saying.

But this episode – if you're scrolling through this in maybe a later week – this episode is called 'New Mexico'. That's not a Bundy-afflicted state, as far as we know, and not where I live, or where we usually record. So why 'New Mexico' and why no guest?

I'll just take a breath here. I need a breath. We need to breathe, right?

Well, as some of you may remember I was born in New Mexico and I only left when I was thirteen. I didn't leave home voluntarily. My dad killed himself. My home exploded out from under me and I was in mid-air. I landed in Colorado.

Without Dad, there was just me – me and New Mexico – so I had to go.

We can never entirely know why people kill themselves. If we know what they intend, we can ask them please to not – *please don't, we need you*. Once they've gone, what can we know? Even if they leave a note, what could they ever say that would explain enough?

I can say that my father died twelve months, to the day, after my mother disappeared. At the time of my father's death, there had been no trace of her found. They located her car eventually, locked up peaceful in a quiet street near the school where she taught. They did not find her.

She went to get ice cream for me. I am why she went out that Saturday afternoon. I wanted Cherry Garcia ice cream because this was 1987 and that was a new and exciting flavour. She did not indulge me in my every whim, that was not our habit, but we'd been getting on really well and having cool times and hanging out and almost, you know, being two women together and friends. So she just said, 'What the hey.' She didn't ever swear that I heard – she was an elementary school teacher and they never swear in the rest of their lives so they won't ever do it by mistake in a schoolroom. 'What the hey. I'll drive into town. I have shoes at the mender's and I'll pick them up and some ice cream and I'll maybe get us Chinese food.' That's approximately what she said. I wish I could remember exactly.

We usually ate healthy, terrific food that she made, but sometimes it's a Saturday and you want loads of fat and sugars and salt and – shout out if you remember this – you want to go to Blockbuster Video and pick up a couple of movies on VHS videotape and physically bring them back to your home, because the Internet is in its infancy and computers weigh as much as a TV and a TV weighs as much as a stocky man of reduced stature holding a bag of bowling balls. Your phone is attached to your house by a physical wire and does nothing but let you make phone calls. So you rent movies.

When someone is missing, you can't call them and ask them where they've gone.

You have no reason to think about that, though, and you plan a nice Saturday evening together with the whole of your family. You don't even plan – you assume. You assume it will happen. We all could have eaten at home and then gone to the local movie theatre. I could have eaten ice cream at the movies. I could have waited to have ice cream some other time, because it doesn't matter.

It wasn't a perfect Saturday morning, it was just usual. It feels perfect now, because I was never going to have another like it. I didn't hug my mother, or tell her goodbye, or that I loved her, because I was reading a Batman comic and she would be back soon, so it's no big deal, just a trip to buy ice cream and do some other stuff.

My mother never got to buy the ice cream. She picked up her shoes. They were inside the car when it was found. The guy in the shoe store remembered her, too, because she was nice.

Be nice, people – then you will be easily brought to mind while increasing numbers of strangers search for you. Your kindness will leave a trail of mild human happiness that anyone can track, although it won't save you. Of course it won't save you – it may even make you disappear.

Dad didn't go with my mother in the car, because he had some invoices to prepare. He was a carpenter. And he had no reason at all to believe that he shouldn't stay at home and do some paperwork, because that would mean a predator would take away his wife and do things to her that never became known.

And that is the kind of thing you would have to kill yourself to forget.

We lived in a pleasant neighbourhood, quiet, West Side of ABQ – Albuquerque – near what was kind of a new golf course then and close to the Petroglyph National Monument and the West Mesa. It made you feel awe. It made you feel that everyone else would experience this awe and be very chilled and contented. And that was almost true – but it only takes one hunter in the forest of your life, yeah?

I went horseback riding sometimes on a little pony called Chopito. He was soft and golden like a Labrador and loved the lady who owned him. It's all so beautiful out there – those mesas are amazing. You want to ride out in it, walk in it – just be close to it. The landscape is stark, but it's lovable, too. My mom would look out sometimes through the kitchen window and she'd say *stark*, either to me or to herself, and that would be a good thing, from the way she said it. She made a garden in the yard – we had this adobe-walled garden. Everything she planted was very soft and I think it was all there to show, when you raised your head, how the world outside was stark but here your home was comfortable. This was her reason for the garden, I think.

In Albuquerque the people are Hollywood overspill and the artsy woo-woo folks – but truthfully those types are more over in Santa Fe. And they've got the adobe vibe, but there's Victorian Gothic, too – it's a mix. There's the native tribes all around there, indigenous land and pueblos, and the breeze from the desert would smell sometimes of being held as sacred. Us wonderful white folks irradiated a sacred site out at Los Alamos, which is near there – as it happens – rehearsing to kill people.

There are some really poor people in ABQ – I guess some *Breaking Bad* people – and the native people are some of the really poor people and I was aware of the poverty, but I didn't have much understanding. The history of the place was messed up and we were taught not so much about it, although my mom explained some things. There was crime in ABQ – there's crime everywhere. There were drugs and drug dealers, back then – mostly I would say there was a whole load of serious drinking, a lot of Vietnam PTSD damage still echoing around. I didn't know much about that, though. We didn't see that in our lives, my mother, my father and me. There were people who had nothing, but none of them hurt us. None of them ever hurt us.

We worried about coyotes maybe killing our cats and I worried about Chopito maybe tripping over in a gopher hole, or a groundhog hole, getting a hoof caught. And sometimes I would worry about people in TV shows fooling around with blank guns like the guy in *Cover Up* – Jon-Eric Hexum – remember him? He shot himself in the head without meaning to, because blanks are still bullets and so you shouldn't fire them into your temple at point-blank range, even if you feel this might amuse a camera crew. And I sort of had this idea that *Moonlighting* was a show like *Cover Up* and that maybe this meant Bruce Willis might do the same thing. I had no other concerns. School was okay, sports were okay, my friends were okay. I worried about Bruce Willis being unaware of basic gun safety.

That Saturday my mom didn't come back for a while and we didn't think much about it. Maybe there was a line in Blockbuster and she was waiting. Maybe she couldn't decide what movies to rent. Maybe she met a friend. She liked talking to friends. There were no cell phones, remember? It was possible to genuinely have no idea where somebody was and their absence would not freak you out for a while.

Only then Mom was away for too long. And my dad started making phone calls and finding out that no one could start doing anything about a missing person for way too long, even if they absolutely should not be missing.

After the phone calls Dad drove out and looked for her, for my beautiful mother, and I sat at home and threw up a lot. I threw up until I had nothing inside, because of the fear I had – which was the start of my throwing-up problem.

I wanted to believe that he would find her, but I couldn't. Somewhere in myself I realised I understood that the world can go bad on you. I had no experience of such a thing being true, but I felt it anyway. And I was guilty for feeling it – like I made things get worse by letting the badness into my thinking.

Dad came home after it was dark and there was no sign of her anywhere he had looked. He hadn't even found the car yet. The police did that later. And I knew it was my fault he hadn't brought her home. I hadn't believed that he could.

We never saw her again.

There was something wrong in every room where she should have been standing, walking, sitting, doing even just the tiny, tiny things she no longer got to do. The house was wrong. The garden was wrong. It all looked the same, but it wasn't. It all ached.

When finally the cops made their first search, they turned up the car – it was parked out at the side of the Adela Sloss Vento Elementary School. It wasn't in the parking lot she'd have used for a trip to the store. We had no idea why. There was nothing wrong with it, no sign of any struggle. Whatever happened, had happened elsewhere is what they told us.

She really loved her school and had helped change its name to commemorate a New Mexican civil rights campaigner. She fought hard for that.

That year later my dad drove the same car into his big workshop which he'd cleaned out the day before. I thought he was doing that to get a fresh start, because I knew the date, too. I remembered the date. You always remember the date when your mother disappears. But he did not want a fresh start, he wanted an end. He gassed himself with exhaust fumes on that same date, so I guess I only have one terrible date instead of two. He gave me that. And he was away from the family home, so I didn't find his body. A guy who came over to talk with him about reconditioning a barn found the body.

Some stranger who wanted to live in a repurposed barn found my father.

I still had to go to the morgue and look at my dad and say who he was, when the police had finished with him. That wasn't so bad as finding the body and it's my opinion that my father thought about who'd find him. He spared me one trouble, even if he couldn't stay. And when I did meet him dead, he was so gone from out of his body that seeing what was left made me think there might be a soul. So much of him was missing that I came to believe in a soul then. Now I think it was just life that was missing, which is a huge thing. Back then I was a kid and being told nothing happens for no reason by people who were offering me religion as if it would help – of course I believed in the soul. Religion kept talking about bringing people back from the dead, but also it didn't do that any more, which made it seem pretty much useless to me – why give up the useful part and hold on to the lousy singing? And what reason could there be for my mother going out to buy me ice cream and never coming home?

All that is how I went to Colorado and started living with my mother's parents. They've passed now, but they were great. They were as great as they could be and I was messed up sometimes and sometimes I was okay. They did their best and the times when I was okay were very much down to them. For a long while I actually thought I was completely okay and then I spent – which I've mentioned on here before – three, four years cutting myself and considering suicide. And there was the throwing up – that lasted ten, fifteen years. And I would want to get life over with and leave, I would consider that.

I actually did Driver's Ed so that I could have a car with which to kill myself, not so that I could have a car to drive. This was more serious than the cutting and the puking, but kind of flew in under my radar, because – as many of you have experienced – your radar gets plenty messed up when a bunch of shit happens and you get some help, but not the right help, and people try what they can to heal you, but it's ineffective. Then you pick lousy boyfriends because – *what if they kill themselves?* You don't want them to be great and then miss them. And you don't want them to be great, because when you kill yourself they will have to miss you. So you choose boyfriends and sexual partners who are a form of self-harm, because then you can govern your pain – you think. All of that.

For the hundredth episode I wanted to tell you about New Mexico. I wanted you to know the details of that: the ice cream and this old blue-green Chevy Monza which didn't kill my mother and did kill my dad and which I had liked because sitting in the back on the big bench seat and surrounded by those weird blue-green panels was like being inside a turtle who loved you and was taking you away to have good times.

And this – what comes next – is what I haven't talked about at all, because of reasons like *therapy takes a while*. I can tell you this now, because of all the solidarity you have offered as humans and women, saying you stand with me and with victims. Your messages every week and meeting you guys when we tour this thing – that all has helped. I don't cut any more, I don't pick up guys who are crazy. I don't puke, not unless I have food poisoning, or stomach flu, or such. I barely, barely drink. I am almost as healed as I can be. Maybe. I need the tattoos, I think. That's pain, but it's art. I believe I deserve art. I don't believe I deserve pain.

The end of the New Mexico story – although these stories don't end – that happens six years ago, a little longer. The end of the New Mexico story is why I eventually started this podcast and why I've made it to one hundred episodes and why I'm going to keep on.

Six years ago – a few months more than that – I get a call, out of nowhere. I get a call from New Mexico. This detective who is called Bronsteen, Bob Bronsteen, tells me that he has been going back through the records of cold cases in the light of new technology and DNA evidence. These days – you are aware – we have the possibility of re-examining samples taken when there was no DNA testing, or when samples had to be sizeable for them to get reliable results. Bob was overseeing a bunch of DNA work. Technical term for multiple DNA analyses – a *bunch*.

Bob also was confronted by this warehouse of physical material, still in storage: jewellery, shoes, clothes, bedsheets, all kinds of samples.

And there were photographs.

And some of you have asked from time to time – *why don't you do a show on the Shutterbug?* The Shutterbug, in case you are unfamiliar, was a coward freak asshole murderer of women. That's all he was. A few women did survive his attempts. For those of you who are not experts, the Shutterbug was a serial killer finally caught in the summer of 1991. That meant he was pretty much entirely overshadowed by the arrest of cannibal freak moron Jeffrey Dahmer. This makes me glad, because he liked attention.

Shutterbug, by the way, was the asshole's own name for himself and surely we don't give them that privilege, we don't give them that oxygen – the murderers who want cute nicknames. We just call every one of them Asshole. Surely, that's what we do? We say – *okay, you're Asshole 87*. That should be all they get. Ever. Would be my opinion. We remember their victims.

Asshole 87 took photographs of his victims. He pretended to be a photographer in order to trap women, abduct women, do what he wanted.

And Bob Bronsteen wants me to fly to ABQ.

You can work out why. It's not hard. You're clever people. You're attractive and intelligent for real.

Bronsteen wants me in ABQ so I can look at some photographs. What are maybe pictures of my mother are in Asshole 87's collection. Asshole 87 kept boxes and boxes of negatives and pictures and some of the women were found alive and some of the faces, the women, were never identified and some of them must be, must be, must be victims, other victims, unrecorded victims.

I hate the word *victim*. There should be a better one. There should be a worse one.

Bronsteen thinks, Bronsteen knows, that my mother was taken by Asshole 87, which is all I'm ever going to call him voluntarily.

While I'm listening to his voice which is a nice and gentle voice, I don't want to understand why Bronsteen knows that. They still have never found her body, my mother's body.

That's the body she did everything with, that she gave a vitamin pill every morning so she'd be healthy and the hair she brushed that smelled of her and her hands and her voice – that's the body that was all of her – that's everything that carried who she was.

Asshole 87's original MO was to approach young girls, nice people, and say he would take their picture, because they were beautiful. He would talk about agents and modelling and dramatic out-of-town locations and photoshoots.

The only thing he didn't lie about was their beauty – all the women he picked were beautiful. They all had gentle eyes.

And his shtick was a corny, creepy shtick which has been used before by other assholes. He was not original. In fact, his MO was so weak and creepy that it didn't often work – not even with relatively innocent young women – not often enough for his need. So he began pretending to be this super pleasant local reporter and could he just, to please his editor, get a snap of you in front of the library where you work, the sports ground you raised funds for, the elementary school you've just had renamed to honour a local heroine ... ?

And fuck him. And why are there experts on his shitty moves and his shitty plans, people who memorise this crap, and there are no experts on my mom, no one but me? Why is that?

I mean, fuck him.

You have to understand ... I mean, I don't understand ...

I'll just say – the soul he hasn't got? Rip it into pieces. Eat it and shit it back out.

Sorry.

Anyway.

I fly to ABQ.

And I go and I meet Bob and sit in the quiet room he has set aside. It's a soft room with a couch, nothing like an interrogation room. And I can tell he is used, by now, to the way this kind of morning may play out. He's calm and he's slow. He gives me space. He gives me agency to go through it in my way. For which I thank him.

And the pictures he has are pictures of my mother.

There she is.

There is some of the time that passed on her last day when I wasn't with her, but she was still alive.

There she is.

She's Mom in all of these pictures that a serial killer had kept.

How he got her, we can't tell, but the pictures suggest, in this horrible way they suggest, the way he did it.

I think it was something like this, although I can't know.

I think that he asked her to help. There are people who always will help and predators look for them. *Oh, you teach there? You were actually involved in the change of name? Well, gee, the paper's just doing a little piece on local facilities and my editor, I know, wants a picture of that very school and it would be great if you were there in the picture. Would you mind? Do you have a little time, ma'am? Well, I know, there were other people involved in it and all, but I'm short of time here. Under the gun. Would you mind? I didn't have time to arrange things and I need to have this written up and a picture by Monday and now it's Saturday and boy am I in trouble. It's more of a general piece, but a real live teacher as well as the school frontage, that would be, just terrific ...*

It was something like that, his trap. It wouldn't have made too much sense, if you paused to think about it, but he would have made it fast and pleading, wounded. She will have been able to tell that he truly was wounded and that would have made her feel obliged. He wouldn't have let her guess the true way in which he was broken.

She would have been in a hurry with ice cream to buy and that trip to get a video or two, but she was nice, so nice, and this wasn't going to take long. This hapless man needed her assistance and it wouldn't take long.

She was so nice.

And, while I was in nurse training I learned this – before I dropped out, I learned this: the minute, infant veins that ran from your umbilical cord into you, from your mother into you – those veins never do go away. They're fanned out and tiny in the wall of your abdomen. Those veins from the time when your blood was the same as your mother's, they're still there. And that's where it hurts you when you finally know that she's gone.

Yes, I flew to ABQ and Bob met me and he was very kind and he'd arranged that very clean and almost domestic room to sit in and this file box with these pictures. Even opening the box was ...

But I do open it and here are the pictures in neat stacks, two stacks of thirty-six pictures with a numbered card on the top of each stack: Number 1, Number 2. And this makes the pictures more frightening – that they're covered by these numbered cards, cut to size – and they always have been frightening, since I've known about them. But I want them, too. I want to see. I'm like a hungry person for them, because this is my mom. This is exactly my mom.

So I pick off the first card and I start looking.

It's funny how you don't often think how much can get in at you when you just have decided you'll keep open your eyes.

There she is.

It was like falling hard so the breath gets kicked out of your chest.

Hi, Mom. Hi, Mom. It's me. It's Phoebe. Oh, Mom.

In the first picture she's being shy and looking sideways into the camera at this monster she doesn't know. She is maybe wondering why they're not quite out front of the school, why they're in this quieter area, why the pictures won't show the new sign. She's thinking. She isn't stupid, not my mom. She's just too kind.

The pictures go in chronological order. Bob has told me they're arranged like that and I can go slowly and stop just whenever I want. He tells me that a lot of times. He wants me to not pick them up all at once.

I don't want to pick them up all at once.

What I want is impossible and none of his business.

You can see as the pictures get taken, my mother has got into the spirit of what he's lied about and said he wants. Teachers join in, they join in first to encourage others. Elementary teachers especially do this because they want small people to trust they can do things in the world, take part and find it fun. In a couple of frames she's reaching her arms out wide in this dramatic gesture and smiling about it at the same time, because she can't take herself seriously as a drama. In some she is pointing at her school as if she's proud of it. She was proud of it.

She's smiling in all of them, these early pictures – different smiles. She is smiling a range of normal human smiles.

And this is one of the beauties of the world. Every smile – every smile I missed – they're all ...

That asshole kept this film, developed these pictures and touched them. He died of cancer on death row in Raiford Prison down in Florida. That isn't enough to make up for touching even one of those pictures, not even that.

He was stupid enough to kill three people, women, human beings, in a death penalty state. Florida: a state where people take pictures all the time, retiree couple pictures, holiday pictures, nice people pictures.

Bob watches me while I lift the next picture of the stack and it shows when my mother's face begins to tense. She has done what he's asked and helped out and why is she still here? Her position has stopped making sense and she's trying to think of polite ways she can leave. Politeness is wonderful for monsters, because it slows you down so they can catch you.

There's a blurry photo where she is beginning to be annoyed and her mouth is asking him something. She's remembering that she's a teacher and she can be firm. In a normal world being firm would work, but she has left civilisation – she is looking in through the lens at someone who has brought somewhere terrible close in around her.

Bob is staying with me all the way through this. He put the pictures into order and he'd seen everything. Having seen everything made his expression strange when he met me.

And he wasn't going to show me the other roll, I was only going to see the pictures from this roll. He told me I could stop at any time.

But you want to keep them company, those people you love. If you can, you have to do that. That's why I didn't stop.

I looked at the other pictures in the second stack.

And you can tell, you can, you can tell – while he's been changing his film and stringing her along with his talking, she has realised this is all wrong. She has made a mistake, a bad mistake. She is thinking quick thoughts and blaming herself. She has been silly. Her face tells you that she thinks she has done something wrong, when nothing is wrong except him.

She has simply been human, acted like a normal human. Only monsters can make that seem silly.

Then in my hand there is the photograph where she sees something very bad, or maybe he has said something very bad to her. She isn't looking into the lens, she is staring at – I don't know what she can see, out there in a side street at the quiet time on a Saturday when people have finished their afternoon, but not yet started evening. There is something bad and she can see it but not understand it – that's how terrible it is. Not understanding is slowing her down when she should run.

But I can't blame her for not running. I think she maybe knows now that she can't and it's too late.

Then she has one hand at her mouth.

I can't tell you.

No one should have to look like that. No one should be able to make them.

And I wasn't there. I was home waiting for ice cream.

And the pictures show he's hitting the shutter release as fast as he can now to catch as much of her going into horror as he can. He does this because he is a monster freak asshole piece of shit.

The last picture Bob lets me see is different. It's the last one in the second stack. You can assume that I'm very emotional by this point. Bob is holding my hand and I don't recall when he started to do that and he doesn't let go until I've stopped crying. He holds on.

And perhaps, when I tell you about the last picture, I'm projecting, trying to find anything to keep me from sucking down carbon monoxide as soon as I can go out and rig up my car. You can think that. Sometimes I think that.

And before I tell you about it, thanks for listening – one hundred episodes. You've helped that happen and you've helped me. You're people who help and together we can be as ready as we possibly can for what happens.

And that last picture is with me for all of my life now. Ink and needles in the skin do not approach that permanence.

My mother is staring right into the lens again and she isn't looking at him. She is so clever and so brave, she is thinking ahead. Her arm is reaching out towards the camera, almost as if she is stumbling, although she's not, and her eyes are wide, wide and blue like desert bluebells. She planted those in her garden. She loved them and in my world they are a sacred thing.

Her arm is reaching and she's looking and it has nothing to do with him, not any more. She has accepted him and what he intends, she can stand knowing something like that and keep on breathing, thinking. She has thrown him away, out of her consideration. He is beneath her. And you can see, I could see, that now she was only hoping that somebody might find these pictures, wishing that in the end someone will find them, somebody other than him. You can see it in her eyes, this hope.

She is acting in the hope that I will see her.

She is looking at me.

Spider

T his morning he'd left seven pebbles outside their front door.

Anne assumed whoever left them was a man. There was a taint of male loneliness about them.

As usual, Anne kicked them off into the gutter before the kids could see. On Saturday morning, she'd slept in, the children and Raph up before her, whoever left the gravel up before them all.

Raph didn't get rid of them. The children would have noticed if he'd come back in and fetched the broom. They'd have wanted to know why he'd start to sweep the street.

It had been gravel yesterday, gravel last Friday, dog shit in a bag on the Monday before, gravel again before that. She'd kept a record of each incident, as if keeping records would make any difference at all.

At least the notes had stopped. The last one was scrawled in a stunted boy's writing on the back of a garage bill. She thought he must have run out of paper, must live in a house where such things were possible. The crumpled bill, twelve Post-it notes, an out-of-season Christmas scene and a flimsy card intended for perhaps an older woman's birthday and then he was done.

Now he was continuing with objects – *Look, look. I'm still out here. I'm still watching. I still hate you. Every morning I can still make you think of me.*

Although, obviously, she doesn't speak Gravel, Stone, Shit. It's simply very easy to be certain of the meaning – they all translate as hatred.

Gravel, Stone, Shit – it sounded like one of those ironic games that grown-ups invent to get childish, to let them get more drunk at parties.

The weather has got no better, was loud all last night. Now the wind is being monstrous in the trees. The big willow down by the river thrashes with outbreaks of silver, upturned leaves like startled fish that can't escape. In other places the radio news has said people are having accidents and power lines are failing – this elongated gale punching in from the Atlantic. The air is warm in a way that's foreboding, dynamic but also oppressive. Autumns are always like this now, it seems.

'The gravel man came.'

Tom, her son, has followed her along the narrow brick entry and is leaning out through the doorway and into the street, inspecting.

Anne stops herself from saying, 'You saw him?' She only cups her hand at the back of Tom's neck, feels that unmistakable delicacy, that extraordinary child skin, the evidence of how we start out clean and soft.

Tom points at the gutter. 'Look. He leaves things.'

So it's sort of okay, then: Tom has only assumed that someone brings the things, that the Gravel Man brings the gravel. She and Raph haven't always moved it far enough away, because they are short of time most mornings. They have missed a trick here. 'It's just stones, gravel – they're all over the place.' When the kids are back at school on Monday she'll be sure to clear everything off with a bucket and shovel. She can dump it on the riverbank, which is where she guesses it has come from.

The neighbours can watch her do it. The neighbours who don't help and yet who must have noticed something can watch and feel ashamed. He may be among them, of course – he may live that close, overlooking, learning the rhythms of the household.

She wants there to be no possibility that her children will want to wait for whoever it is, look out for the mystical Gravel Man. She'll remove every trace and go in to give the afternoon tutorials in a good mood, be especially patient.

Tom is still examining the stones, his posture thoughtful in a way that seems inappropriate for someone who is seven. He is named after the philosopher Thomas Aquinas, who was a thinker. She can't complain if he's growing in that direction. Aquinas was also a saint. That's a lot to live up to.

You have to name things carefully, be cautious about words. You don't leave them in filth on a doorstep.

'The gravel's like leaves.' She lies to her son with hope-fully jovial firmness. 'No one brings the leaves. They just arrive. Things get everywhere.' *Things get everywhere.* This is an incredibly shoddy explanation – the sort of thing her father might have said.

She doesn't entirely meet Tom's eyes while she steers him inside and closes the passage door, shuts it hard so that the lock clicks, the swollen wood of the frame resisting and then giving in. She is perfectly sure that her son is pondering how leaves are very light and gravel is heavy and can't be blown about. Every day Thomas is more Thomas.

Both her children are intelligent – and not in the usual manner of academics' offspring: those tiny, awful performing-bear children – the miniature professors that she comes across in other lecturer mothers' kitchens. Tom and Deborah are miniature people, real human beings, just themselves, authentic. They have these strange veins running through them, ideas that emerge from nowhere predictable.

They have tangible hearts.

When they sleep she can hover her palm above their cheeks, she can kiss them and already feel the good heat in their hearts, the bright heat.

She hugs her arms down over Tom's shoulders, scoots in behind him, while they walk along the whitewashed brick entry and back into the courtyard which is their garden. It's nicely placed between the crooked walls of other houses, not besieged, just held.

Anne hears the back door of their house swing inward and hit the kitchen wall as she rounds the corner of their home. They own the door, they own the house – it's theirs. And this should be a good thing and they should be happy.

'It was the blowing.' Her daughter's voice calls from inside to explain. There is a round dent in the plaster where the interior doorknob impacts once a week or so, sometimes more.

'I know. It's very windy. Don't come outside. You might blow away.' Anne loves the way they call to each other. They don't need to be always together, to cling, but it's nice to stay in earshot.

Deborah is standing in the kitchen doorway, her hands caged around something and a shine of excitement about her. Tom runs to stand beside his sister, clapping his hands against his thighs in excitement. It's clear they both understand what's inside Deborah's fingers. Anne hopes it is not a stone, not gravel. She doesn't want either of her children to have touched something the Gravel Man has touched.

The door bangs again, but gently.

'What do you have there, then?' Anne ushers them back into the kitchen, closes the house behind them, registers The Dent. It's not very much worse, it's just The Dent.

The Dent was already there when they moved in and Anne is fond of it. It means that other families have lived here and made mistakes, other families haven't minded small things going wrong, other families have undoubtedly raised children in the four bedrooms which would give any couple room for children and maybe also guests. She and Raph and Deborah and Tom have got out of the city and are breathing clean air and their garden is hugged in by a Georgian wall, their own Victorian walls, another Georgian wall, a mysterious wall full of thin red bricks and flints. They've bought a whole house with their Leaving London money and The Dent is proof of its continued and settled use, a symptom of survival.

The children are whispering to each other while they glance at her.

I live in a happy, happy home. We run up and down the stairs and we pat the walls and we say nice things to our house. We love it so that it will love us back.

Her love for The Dent, the house, is tantamount to superstition, to something she shouldn't approve of, because it speaks of fear. Really, though, it's only that the children enjoy their new surroundings and like talking to them.

Hello, House. Sleep well, House. Good morning, House.

They are a family and now have a family tradition.

One son, one daughter – exactly what we wanted, not planned, because there are things you can't plan. One daughter, one son is exactly right. Look at them being just exactly right. This bit has to be good, because we deserve it. This bit has to be good, because their future will be hard.

If they want to take part in the children's strikes on Fridays when they're older we will support that. I discussed it with Raph. We think it's very likely that they'll want to change the world.

A few of the notes from the Gravel Man took exception to the fact that Raph had fathered children.

BREEDING MORE BASTARD TRATORS.

The Gravel Man read as ignorant, as clinging on to preformed madnesses, unable to quite repeat their original phrasing. Thick printing with a shake in the letters from unknown sources – it stank of paranoia and websites, of failing and hating it.

WE ARE THE WATCH COMMITTEE.

Gravel Man surely longed to have a uniform and absolving permissions to act.

WE SEE YOU.

Anne hates the way she remembers every sentence. Bad sentences don't have the right to be memorable.

'Look.' Deborah's face is all discovery and importance. She was named after Deborah the warrior and prophet and lawyer. She can pick one, pick them all.

It's odd how children can outgrow the most grandiose aspirations.

Little boy child, little girl child – look at you.

'We found it underneath the honeysuckle.' Tom gives this a triumphant emphasis, appropriate for someone who has just uncovered Troy.

Or one of those bloody Victorian explorers we're all supposed to worship, scribbling English names across other people's landscapes.

The kids are always finding things underneath things and this is a good sign, but she sometimes wonders –

Dear God. Shit.

Warrior Deborah lifts one hand up off the other and right here now is a spider of prodigious size.

'I see. Yes. A spider. That's nice.'

Shit, shit, shit.

Anne says the correct things for the occasion. 'It doesn't really live inside, though. I mean, it wouldn't make a good pet.' She hopes these are the correct things.

'We have spiders living inside, though. There's one in the bathroom.' Thomas, the scholar's friend, is not wrong.

Anne is waiting for Raph to deal with the bathroom spider, or for herself to deal with it, or for it to go away spontaneously, or just die – she isn't quite sure which plan will be most successful.

Shit.

Anne wants to save her daughter's hand from the spider, knock to the floor and then hit it with her shoe, but doesn't because this would set a bad example. 'I don't think the bathroom spider wants a friend.'

The creature is possibly bracing itself a little, like a freshly revealed contestant on a game show. It seems spry, seems confident, seems like a part of a place that's appalling and now closer.

Superstitious. Just a spider. Never liked them, that's all. Just never liked them.

And why bring it in here? And why not be scared of it? Scared of spiders is normal.

She is proud of her children, inquisitive children, but also you need to have natural fears to keep you safe.

And she wants to know why her children always find things underneath things.

Do they always look down? Does that mean they are sad? Has the bastard, bastard Gravel Man made them sad?

She tells them, 'I think it might even eat the bathroom spider.'

Her children's expressions grow more intent and, no, they are certainly not sad. 'Eat him?'

'Yes. If we put her in the bathroom, will she eat the other spider?'

Shit, it's so bloody huge.

They gaze at her with this expression which is becoming increasingly frequent – the one which no longer believes she knows everything. 'I ... No. She, or he, would like to be outside where there are lots of things a spider likes to eat.'

'They could get married.' Deborah peers at the spider as if this will help her to know about the spider's preferences. She expects the world to show her things and be rational. This is wrong, but is probably necessary.

'Spider babies!'

Dear God, no.

We don't believe in God.

Why aren't they afraid?

'I think it's a bit late in the year for them to marry.'

'Or have a civil ceremony.' Thomas's latest fascination. His year teacher is some kind of mild bigot – it will be a problem soon.

British spiders don't bite. Except these days it's hot enough for worse spiders. False widows. We can have false widows.

Moving to the country involves spiders.

The thing begins rearing about on her daughter's hand. It has purpose.

There aren't any false widows in the village – Helen in the post office would have said.

Anne tries to sound like somebody who doesn't want to crush the thing now, now, now. 'We've said hello, though, and it's time to take it back to its home.' The children look unwilling in a way that may become dogged. She doesn't want to have an argument about this, definitely no shouting and invoking of rules. It's Saturday – shouting and rules on a Saturday is hopeless, it ruins Sunday with all the repetitive mentions of fun you could be having but are not, because of misbehaviour.

Oh, Christ.

In whom we don't believe, but it's an expression …

The thing begins blithely rappelling down off Deborah's palm towards the kitchen floor – fast, fast, fast – fat body glistening like a liquid, needle feet.

It'll run under the cooker – shit.

'He likes us.' Tom says this, bending forward, slides his hand into the space under the spider and catches it in his palm. He has the air of someone who has done this a good deal, which is odd of him, strange of him.

Not having dived in before Tom and caught a christingly huge spider to spare her children now makes Anne a bad mother.

Not very bad, but bad.

'Shall we just – don't let it go on the floor – shall we take it back outside to where it lives?' Tom is now playing with it, letting it drop from hand to hand, frustrating its attempts to head for darkness and a place where it can lay eggs, or do something less natural. 'I bet it wants to go home.'

But Tom and Deborah just keep on watching the thing being busy-legged and pseudo-mechanical. Anne also has to watch, but doesn't share their fascination.

It is good they're not scared. We read them Charlotte's Web *to make sure they weren't scared. We did a good job.*

Both children have been taught about liking things and kindness in general. They are fearless and there is no fear in kindness. But their curiosity now doesn't seem like kindness.

But, they're fine, they're soft. They wouldn't hurt a thing, not even a spider.

Tom smiles at her and needs a haircut and is himself – a boy who is funny and ridiculously patient about personal projects involving crafts and surprisingly polite. Today he has also clearly realised that his mother is scared while he is not.

A new off-kilter glimmer shows in both children's faces.

'It has lots of legs.' Deborah says this as if it has come as a revelation to them both, when that's not true at all. They have already learned about spiders in a fair amount of detail – all kinds of arachnid facts.

Deborah isn't being factual – her tone suggests that the number of legs is a challenge.

The children exchange a clouded grin and it's somehow plain they've talked about making a spider have fewer legs. They might not take all of them, but some. Perhaps that.

'Lots and lots, lots of legs.' Tom softly blames the spider for being itself, dropping it, hand over hand. It looks like a bleak obsession manifested, glinting. It looks like a corruption.

Anne hates the spider and does want to kill it herself, but she doesn't want a thing which is alive being harmed by her children.

Her children's easy handling of the creature becomes suddenly suspicious, reprehensible.

You can't be with them every minute like a warden. You can't always know.

And a glare of sun strikes in through the kitchen window and the spider's body turns in it, immaculate, and the fine baby curls at Deborah's temples shine pale and she reaches out to put her hand on her brother's shoulder and Tom's fingers move, cleverdelicate, like a tender man's, and nothing bad happens, not a thing.

The children begin to go outside as if they had always meant to and Anne follows. Tom's hand is high, the spider swaying beneath it, dropping slowly. Anne notices that she's exhaling – that she had been clinging on to her breath.

My children don't hurt things. It would show.

I would have hurt it, but that's different – I'm an adult and an adult's a lost cause.

'Will she still be there to play with tomorrow?' Tom lets the spider drop onto his sister's hand.

'Maybe.'

Deborah has just enough time to say 'Goodbye' before the spider plummets again, lands free and disappears itself into the honeysuckle's depths, legs so fast they seem to writhe. So this tiny trace of horror will always be there now, a darkness in the dark beneath each leaf, a potential.

I liked that honeysuckle.

Outside the nice walls, red brick and flint and lime mortar walls, there is the Gravel Man. He must live quite close, surely – definitely in the village. She maybe passes him in the street. The Gravel Man mentioned when Raphael got a new coat, referred to it the day after. What the Gravel Man is inside doesn't show. It should, but it doesn't show.

He makes her study faces: village acquaintances, half-familiar strangers, the solitary backs that walk away when she opens the door to the street.

They all look equally innocent, equally guilty.

And rubs her forearms, as if this will remove the chill of spiderness. 'She'll want to make a new web somewhere and catch things for her dinner.'

'Flies!'

'Flies!'

Anne has no idea why this is a glorious idea, why it makes them leap around on the paving stones, waving their arms.

'Flies! Flies! Flies!'

They are happy, definitely happy. The wind seems to lift them higher than would be usual.

They won't blow away, though. They won't do that.

The Gravel Man barely exists for them. And no one has given them trouble at school – just that one conversation about beliefs with Tom's teacher. Everyone has beliefs – there's no need for them to insist other people share them.

Raph hardly has an accent – he sounds more English than some English people.

That's Germans for you, Anne – we sound more English than the English and we look more English than the English.

He used to say this a lot and laugh about it, add that he has an ancestral gift for assimilation: Kurdish father moving and moving and worse than moving, Jewish mother whose mother remembered moving and moving and worse than moving. Since the notes, he doesn't speak about these things. He speaks less altogether. The Gravel Man doesn't look at Professor Raphael White and see an Englishman in corduroys and a flat cap, a Harris tweed jacket with tailoring that's too crisp. That's from Cologne. The Gravel Man sees a FILTHY JEW GERMAN ISIS CUNT. Raphael has a doctorate, is a professor – YOU'RE NOT A DOCTOR LYING SHIT. YOU WANT TO KILL US ALL.

She's started to wish that Raph could be taken as safely Caucasian, Christian Caucasian. This is a racist kind of wish, a squeeze of other people's thinking changing her mind.

Anne wants Raph to be at home now. He won't be long, but she wants him now.

I know what that means – you want to kill us all – it means that the Gravel Man's longing to get his kill in first.

It always means the same.

But Raph will be home soon. He's off foraging. He's in love with farm shops, farmers' markets and boxes of eggs and potatoes left at the roadside on tables with honesty boxes. '*I shall forage and return.*'

He still says that.

We're not afraid.

We're not afraid for ourselves.

We all eat fresh local produce, we go for country walks.

We have a crime number.

I keep a record of each incident.

'Do you know what?' She is surprised by her voice, how normal and domestic it still sounds. 'I think I'm going to bake biscuits.' She raises a cheer from her children who then continue to be flies, or flying things. 'They'll probably be oat and honey and if you are both extremely perfect you can maybe eat one each while they're warm and floppy.'

'Like rabbit's ears!' Tom wants a rabbit almost as much as Deborah wants a dog. For security reasons they're considering a dog. She and Raph worry, though, about how to make a dog distrustful enough of strangers and still gentle with the kids. Anne thinks that if the dog really loves the children, loves the family, then it will defend them, no matter what. Love does that.

Anne decides she'll have a bath first and wash off the shiver of the whole spider episode. Then she'll bake – biscuits are quick – and then Raph will be home.

And I'll wash away the Gravel Man.

Tom's hair flares up in the shapes of flames. 'Do the legs grow back?'

'Nothing ever grows back.'

The children may not have heard her. They have opened their arms straight and are letting the wild touch of nothing suggest they're in flight.

'Well, you have fun, you two. Shout if you need me. Biscuits soon. Don't let the door bang if you come in.'

She trusts them outside alone. They won't do anything cruel.

And she'll walk upstairs and bath in the clean, new family bathroom with the hammam towels, because hammam towels are softer and they dry fast on the rail and don't get musty. And then she'll bake. And then she'll call her children and hug them and feed them a little.

After that Raph will be home and she'll hug her husband and look at what he's brought back from the autumn: apples, blackberries, eggs, turnips, honey, pumpkin, sprouts, those kinds of things.

Things just get everywhere.

He's careful to find things that are good. He has a good eye.

We are watching.

Anne hates, more than anything, the way in which a stranger, a cowardly and pitiful stranger, can make your life seem a breakable pretence, something that's shallow and a pantomime because you don't deserve it and can't own it, can't really own anything.

HOW CAN YOU BE A JEW'S WHORE? ISIS BRIDE WHORE.

WE SEE YOU WITH YOUR FILTHY MIXED KIDS BLACK BITCH.

WE SEE YOU WITH YOUR JEW PIMP.

HOW CAN YOU FUCK A RAGHEAD KRAUT?
WE SEE YOU.

There's no *we* – Anne knows that. Whoever the Gravel Man is, he's alone. There are many more like him, but they're all alone.

Somehow, she still hasn't gone inside – is letting the breeze race her mind clean, is watching her beautiful children, her children and Raphael's children, calling her safe, well, gentle children. 'Actually, kids – Debs, Tom – come and give Mum a cuddle. She needs a cuddle.'

They come to her quickly – they're becoming bored with flying – and she gathers them in tight. Barely a thought can slip in between them.

YOUR FILTHY MIXED KIDS.

'And now I'm going to phone your father and ask him how his foraging is getting on and I will listen to him being happy about parsnips and you can say hello, too, and we'll tell him not to be away much longer because we really, really miss him, don't we? Yes, we do.'

She does go in, does gather the kids and go in, and then she does call Raph. He is happy about kale. Deborah tells him about the spider and Tom tells him again. Neither of them mentions how many legs it had. They speak of it fondly with simple excitement.

She takes charge of the phone again. 'Sweetheart, come back fairly soon, though.' The weather is raging against the receiver wherever he is and she can hardly hear him.

'One last farm ...' Raph loves his produce hunting, his ability to eat a connection with the ground beneath his feet. '... home.'

'I know, but soon.'

'I saw the stones.' And the greyness in his voice is very clear, clearer than the words.

'I know.'

'I kicked them away. Not enough, but away. I would have ...' He isn't angry, only grey. And his weather is racing, raging.

'I saw. Come home.'

In a brief outbreak of stillness, she hears him say, 'Are you okay?'

He asks this a lot now – ever since he opened the first note. He unfolded it while walking through the passage to the garden. Then he punched the wall. Then he punched it again. He left blood on the whitewashed brick, apologised, washed it off and kept on scrubbing.

It's not that he can't be angry, it's that he was deciding against it. He was constructing a better plan. They are both trying to do that. They are intelligent people – they must be able to find a solution to utter stupidity.

'I'm fine. Bring me my kale and my husband. Bring me my husband happy and well and triumphant.' Saying this because the Gravel Man can't win and can't be in all their conversations.

Something like a press of breath rises against the receiver, unsteady and then easing. 'I am almost on my way.' He pauses again, preparing to be happy for her. 'I will be garlanded with sprouts.'

Raph has a warm imagination – they both do. They both earn a living by solving problems with imaginative grace. This should be applicable to any situation.

'I'll stay right here.' And she doesn't add – *because Gravel Man isn't your fault. He is his own fault. He can't make us go small.*

'I am glad you will stay right there.' He stalls again and allows her to hear birdsong, harsh and near him, distorting in the endlessness of the breeze.

She holds the phone tight to her head even after the call is over. This continues the contact in a way which is superstitious and based in unbridled fear.

Raph checks the tyres for nails. We always do, after that one time.

Then she walks from room to room, goes into every room and turns on every light.

As she goes, the children follow, her certainty drawing them on.

He wants to kill us.

'Let's switch all the lamps on, shall we? Let's make the whole of the house shine so that everyone can see us being happy when the dark comes. We won't close the curtains and they'll all look and they'll know that we're happy.'

She understands the sunset is hours away. She understands she is performing a kind of ritual, a series of acts that may be senseless.

At the moment, this is all she can think of to do.

'When the dark has come, they'll know that we are here.'

We Are Attempting to
Survive Our Time

It's like that moment – you know the moment – when your hero is trapped with your villain – the one who's killed before – and their eyes meet. You understand that things will all kick off now – in this cable car, lift, museum, cathedral, or other location of visual or murderous interest. There are wonderful depths here into which one could hurl bodies, or lovely walls off which one might bang heads. There may possibly be ornamental and iconic whatnots, set ready to bludgeon or pierce should a rapid mind deploy them with violence.

This is a familiar scenario and something we're all used to.

And there's always this gaggle of schoolkids, nuns or elderly eccentrics who interrupt. They burst in upon the scene and halt the moment. The coming injuries hold their breath and tight little smiles are forced. Hostilities are suspended whenever an audience enters – that's the rule. But I am here and so is he and so is our audience and our smiles are completely exhausted and we're still fighting.

We are both alert and circling up at the top, or quite close to the top, of Cologne Cathedral. We have climbed inside one of its towers, all the way to this high room where we are being watched by dozens – approximately dozens; I don't really have time to count – of witnesses. Still, we're not stopping, we're not even slowing down. While his arms swipe in the air above him, another string of breathlessly happy Italians is emerging from the narrow doorway at the top of the winding Christ-this-is-endless staircase. Heads first and then hands slapping the last steps, up they struggle. Each one of them stares and flinches as soon as they notice us. Or rather, as soon as they see the source of all those yells they kept on hearing while they made their ascent. We are making Italians flinch.

We keep on yelling, because we can't stop.

I would say Tom is, to be more accurate, howling.

We are being loud Brits, the kind anyone might assume are already drunk and anxious to eat more chips. We aren't absolutely the villains here, but also we aren't doing well. The Italians divide, some retreating to simply descend again, some hurrying past us, as if we're a small fire, and heading for the upper, final level and the observation deck. No one seems to have any intention of intervening in what is not a thrilling confrontation between theatrical superspies, but something shoddy and domestic. We are an appalling couple screaming only in English and nevertheless creating inter-national offence.

Tom is screaming at me, my Tom. And I am screaming back.

Two Japanese girls were already here when we arrived. We were mildly distressed by the climb, then, but peaceful. It seems they're both going to sit through our display: his rising irritation, my rising irritation, his wheeling arms, my folded arms, the words and words and words. They're watching from the wide stone ledge built around whatever this room is – an ecclesiastical room near the top of a tower – one that doesn't have bells. We've seen the one with bells. Everybody in here must have seen the one with bloody bells – it's halfway up, you can't avoid it. The sane people stop there and then go back down.

In the bell room – belfry? – we didn't hate each other. We hadn't potentially traumatised two young women, one of whom has folded her knees up in front of her with an air of seeking shelter. In the hotel, around five hours ago, I had no idea we would come to this. I doubt it's what she expected, either.

Maybe Tom did expect it, though. Things have been odd between us, or brisk, or tense, or something else uncomfortable for a while. Then again, at home everybody is uneasy. People these days hesitate, avoid every trace of inflammatory subjects, almost any subjects. They talk about weather forecasts and TV shows, tiptoe and murmur with strangers, improvise opinions about sports. It's fashionable to feel threatened and confined. Equally, out in the streets, people are screaming, screaming in English – screaming into phones, into nowhere, into known and unknown faces. It's all made us feel disheartened, to be frank. Tom and I were close to being frightened of the screamers, but glad that we weren't like them. Here we are ourselves, though – screaming, screaming, screaming. We're just the same.

Tom is louder than me, of course.

Men are louder. That's a generalisation, but he is making me generalise. It's his fault.

As a couple we've tried to avoid being simple about the sexes, the orientations. We try to take people as people. We aim to be kind. And when it comes to the sexual clichés, we met in our maturity, didn't have kids, so many of them have never affected us.

We're both generalising now, though. You can't yell in nuances; it doesn't feel right.

I wasn't the villain when we were still looking at the bells. Up here I am all of the bad things about women.

I am holding back and being the better person, because women are flexible and compromise. While I'm being better than him, it's impossible not to know that Tom's being exactly, typically, disappointingly like a man and I do have to say that. I'm just letting the words turn red, be this wonderful push of heat and mindlessness. It's not unpleasant. It breaks a sweat.

It's terrible. It makes me the worse person. It's not true about Tom, but Tom's being not true about me. It's all too confusing not to keep on, keep on shouting.

And now he's yelled *that*.

Tom said *that*. *That*.

And meanwhile, squeezing out from between the rubbed-smooth stonework is a man not built to shove himself up stairwells designed for those of medieval stature.

That.

Whenever I want to kiss you on the cheek your mouth's in the way.

Tom said *that*.

My Tom.

I can't look at him. I can't watch him being like this. I turn and face the new arrival, try to smile in a civilised way at him. I may be yelling, but I'm civilised. The man's broad shirtfront is very wet and maybe the shock of us will push him clear over some terrible cardiac edge.

That.

Tom and I would both be unhelpful in the event of an emergency. We'd make a good effort, but we are in a careless mood.

Who in the hell would say *that* to anyone?

And I am not anyone – I am me. I am bloody well me and he knows me and who I am.

And very, very quickly it is clear to me this is not the moment when the villain meets the hero, but their fight is delayed by a crowd of interlopers. This is the moment when the woman slaps the man. This is one of those scenes where the man is inexcusable and a crowd is there to know it and bear witness. Then the woman rushes out and has her reasons for it and the man gets considered, judged, found wanting by multiple observers. And possibly somebody overweight starts having a heart attack.

We would all help him. We wouldn't let him die.

And I can't slap Tom. Slapping anyone is inexcusable and Tom is Tom and I know Tom. I can't hurt him.

Even though it was inexcusable to say *that*.

And the moment for doing anything has gone. My feeling was only a feeling and has gone, is practically gone, and nobody ought to get hit and nobody should hit them. This is a generalisation, but also true outside of medical emergencies and warfare, specific humanitarian situations.

A grey-skinned woman in a jovial baseball cap is helplessly staring at us.

This may be because Tom is swearing and may be because I have been swearing, too. We are good at swearing. At home we've been known to do it just for fun. We have a skillset and are effing and blinding, as my grandma would have said, right up in the heights of a house of God.

Tom is detailing all of the ways in which I am peculiar and inappropriate in public. I attempt to list some of the ways in which he is bizarre, unapproachable and punitively bleak.

We're not inaccurate. We're also not right.

I want to stop this. We ought to stop this. Neither of us is going to, though, and I can't think how today will end – that, or I don't want to.

Under our feet is the long, hollow reach of the tower and then the redbluegold of glass light, dropping onto flagged floors, droop-headed people in pews and the prayer-glow of organised candles. Down there is an arching vault full of little whispers, up here it's all swearing.

Up here we don't know what we were thinking and can't understand and never and always and wouldn't and can't – nothing means that much, but we can feel the music.

And Tom has this one curl at the back of his neck. I've only just seen it – one curl among all the straight and straightish strands, one curl nestled in tight to itself. He must have missed it with the comb this morning – this morning when all was well – seemed well – and we weren't both *weird, despicable, stupid, perverse, unfeeling, a shit*. Or else, we were, but didn't have to say so.

The curl is very beautiful. Every time he turns – pacing, high-armed and long-fingered, as if he's conducting himself – it's possible to see the curl.

I don't want baseball cap woman to ever notice it. She wouldn't think well of him for it, would assume that he is careless.

From what there is of her expression she could be assuming that we're an attraction here, an arguably blasphemous floor show to crown the ascent. She might leave us an online review – four stars. I don't think we could merit a five-star review, not really – it's not as if we're making any efforts to be entertaining, we're shedding no blood, although there is the swearing which should give us credit in an age obsessed with shocks.

Only, to me, this feels like bloodshed.

We aren't being filmed, at least. That is, I don't think so. Everybody has some kind of camera, apart from the homeless. Millions of lenses are ready to film screams and cruelty, make sure they spread.

I feel sick. This may be because of the tremble in the stone beneath my feet. I could be sure that we're going to somehow plummet, Tom and I, swing away from each other in the fall and only land when we are miles and miles apart. We would never get home. We would never be home. Perhaps we've said too many words, perhaps now we're worse and worse people, incurably.

And outside I know there are grey-stone angels perching, modelled with curtailed, art deco wings, bare feet, faces sufficiently blank and terrifying, empty-eyed enough to seem a realistic depiction. They're trapped up here: those wings would never bear their weight.

Tom and I find issues about broken ornaments and texts and we have different interpretations of what is reasonable, or common sense, and there are so many, so many, so many things wrong with us. We are awful and unreasonable and we take to it like knives. I want to ask him how deep we can drop and still survive?

I see the curl again, the pinch of sweet hairs held soft, the curve resting on his collar.

And then I don't know why we've stopped. Tom has stopped. I've stopped. We're quiet. The peace aches, rings. His feet are planted flat, the rest of him arising like an inevitability. I used to love the way he did that – the way he took up his exact amount of space. He could have been poured upwards, against gravity – that's the suggestion his body makes.

Are we tired, exhausted, frightened of ourselves? I never have understood fighting, what it does to who you are. Tom has been louder than my father, louder than the loud man I was with after my father, louder than anyone. Still, I'm not afraid of him, he doesn't contain any cause for it, not anywhere. It's what I'm like that's worrying me.

My first fight when I've fought back. I could be proud of myself, but I'm not. And I shouldn't have been with anyone, even Tom, who can casually say *that*.

We're nowhere near high enough for thin air, but we're both out of breath.

The smaller of the Japanese girls is hugging her stomach – as if whatever we are has affected her womb. I feel she is being melodramatic.

We haven't affected *my* womb. Too late for that. Tom and I have had to be each other's children.

And today we've made ourselves a spectacle, been more than childish. We've no dignity. You're supposed to be more comfortable with dignity – like somebody wearing galoshes when it rains. Only nobody actually wears them any more and dignity is also dated where we come from, in the same way having food is passé, or wanting a future without empty eyes, pointless wings, bad angels.

Our country is packed with ideas no one should say. You need somebody who'll stay with you in a place like that.

I could swear all our observers are leaning closer in this silence. They're greedy for us, for more excitement. The stones around us feel impatient.

Tom and I aren't breaking up.

Are we breaking up?

I can't tell if we feel that way.

And I don't know how we'd manage another night here being in the same hotel room, the same bed. The flight home has our seats booked, seats together. His other shoes are in my bag and will not fit in his bag, because he won't ever travel with an adequate size of bag. And the whole of our everything waiting back there in splintered Britain, little island, can't be unpicked.

Tom reaches and holds my hand. I hold his.

He starts again.

This time his yelling sounds horrified, not hateful, which is sort of good. It could mean that he doesn't hate me. It also could mean I'm horrifying.

His hand keeps holding on.

It sounds as if he's shouting spells: strong ones to make me show myself, how terrible I'll be. I know he's always chosen women who will hurt him. I hadn't quite seen until now that he always expects to be harmed and gets tired of waiting. He has picked women who would be quick. I have been a mistake.

I am a woman who wanted to slap him, but I didn't. I did not. An idea is nothing, not unless you listen to it.

I wouldn't be with him if I believed I wasn't safe – safe in both directions.

His hand is tight round mine and he looks so scared and he keeps on, shouting past me at other partners, other times, a confusion of intimate humiliations. His eyes aren't quite asking me how I'll destroy him, but it's something like that.

His touch seems desperate, or injured, or resigned.

I hold on while the past falls through him.

Your actions count, not your thinking – your actions are out in the world, not in your head. We understand that.

What you are in the world is a choice and you don't think a vile thing and make it more vile and then do it. In the end, no one could bear that. We've talked about the way that peace used to be agreed and commonplace. We're thoughtful people who ought to be able to work things out. We used to touch hands and barely notice, kiss and barely notice, but it meant something good all the same.

Tom faces me, Tom who is still Tom.

And I wish I could walk right into his earlier life and mend it, ease it. I wish I could mend my own past. I wish Tom wasn't still shouting, I wish that I knew what I ought to do next, what I could do. I wish that we lived in a merciful country. I can wish anything that I like, but wishes are useless. They're popular but they don't work, they're feral dreams and you should keep away from them.

If wishes were horses then beggars would ride. If wishes were horses then there would be horses everywhere: in living rooms, in sleeping bags, in hospitals, in graveyards, there would be so many horses. I'd take Tom the length of our street at home and we'd hold hands, watch the horses passing.

He has opened a crack in his voice.

I know that he can't be alone with himself – that would leave him with someone he can't like. You never are alone; you're with yourself, that's always the problem. I'd seek out solitude if it weren't for that, if it weren't for the soft curl in his hair.

When he next takes a breath I will tell him something, I have to find something, something, something to fix us, if we can be fixed. I'd like him to see how tiny we are, inside everything, inside reality, and that we should always make sure we're all right. Tiny, tiny. Gentle, gentle. You have to be gentle when you're so small.

But before I can say anything, here it comes at last: he tells me I am like his mother. I remind him of his mother. I am just like his mother.

Finally.

That's done, then.

He never has said this before, but it's always been with us, like a mournful or else predatory shadow on our walls.

He is looking at me with this animal surprise and I am smiling, while our pasts gallop by like horses.

I tell him that he isn't my dad shouting and he isn't that other sod shouting, isn't the sod who came after him, or the bastard before. He isn't a link in the chain-link fence of sods and bastards. I didn't pick him to keep my life tiring and then more than tiring. He isn't the other men, or anything like them. I say something like that.

And I won't hurt him and he won't hurt me and we are tiny, tiny, gentle, gentle.

Then we speak some more, we name our wounds and sins and we do this very quietly and I suppose this is appropriate for our location.

He hasn't gone. Neither have I. Like a miracle, but not.

A family of Germans vanish themselves up the metal steps that lead to the outdoor level and possibly haven't noticed that we're here. The fat man is studying his hands. The baseball cap woman – I'm not sure where she went.

I look at the Japanese girls and I raise Tom's hand in mine just slightly, as if we are a trophy. The gesture feels slightly ridiculous, but the motion finds an echo. We begin to swing our hands upwards and forwards, downwards and backwards, softly.

I don't know if the girls understand all of the obscenities we have used. I hope not, although I'm doubtful – obscenities travel so well. I smile at them and they both look at me as if I'm a criminal, one of a pair.

I keep smiling, nonetheless, and Tom and I swing our arms higher and faster, like schoolgirls being excited on an outing. Tom is smiling, too. Our absence of yelling makes the ceiling seem further away.

Outside among the spires there are saints carved, holding aloft objects of lost meaning. We aren't going to inspect them.

I listen to the pairs and chords of footfalls, descending, ascending. The next visitors emerge from the tight whirl of time-concaved steps and modestly sanctified air. Tom and I wheel to face them, proprietorial. After all, we must have been here much longer than average. It may be that we look quite innocent to them and normal, although I doubt it.

The fat man produces a watery grin for us and leans his head back to touch the wall behind him, shuts his eyes.

I'm pretty sure he won't die today and leave a monumental corpse, impossible to thread down a spiral staircase. We won't be *Rage Couple in Cathedral Death* or *Heart Shame Screamers*. He'll be quite safe and we won't be broken in various multimedia ways. We'll be broken for other reasons, later – it happens to everyone – but we won't break each other. I don't think we'll break each other.

And tiny, tiny and gentle, gentle we begin an embrace which is oddly difficult, unwieldy. I listen at the height of Tom's heart, fit my cheek against his being alive. I do not tell him now, but will later, that I have never known how to have an argument. The fighting has always come from someone else and I have kept my head down, because I like my head and I don't like bloodshed. Being hurt all the time gets too much after a while. The best I have ever done is to run away.

Today no one is bleeding. Today something went wrong, but then changed for the better and didn't immediately collapse. We neither of us expect that, not any more.

It would also appear we're no longer alone and no longer pretending, no longer preparing to run. That's probably true. It's nice.

Our last witness, the large man, opens his eyes again and stands with a little sigh, before telling us something which probably means *Goodbye*. There's certainly the feel of parting in it. Tom and I probably offer him the blanked expressions of polite concussion patients everywhere. He is light-footed in the way that substantial people often are. Perhaps he only stayed to stop us murdering each other, thought he could help.

As we follow him towards the doorway, I could swear the tower shifts again, and that candle flames must be shuddering, row on row, in Kölner Dom. It will make the tourists feel unsteady.

We're tourists ourselves.

Finally descending, we lean against the greasy stone spindle at the narrowest edge of the steps. We have no choice, because those who are climbing, and therefore suffering, monopolise the safer, broader way beside the wall. We are going back down to the world where suffering makes everyone uneasy and unsafe, but we have to keep moving along and pretending this isn't the case.

I look at his curl of hair, feel our mutual concern at every vague stumble. Tom has gone first because then I can land on him if I trip. I have pointed out I'd most likely kill him when I did. We go on anyway, sinking, the sharp turn of the spiral dizzying.

Out in the open air, we walk round the main bulk of the cathedral. It reeks of specialness and holy resins. We give the beggars euros until we have no euros left, because this seems the proper thing to do, but still there are more beggars. It isn't comforting to imagine the beggars have always been here, kneeling and keening for help over centuries. They fail to seem a period feature, need being perpetually in the present tense.

Tom and I are lucky and we know it. We walk under our luck like a type of shame, a heaviness. We have money, our country still has intact buildings in most places, intact homes, no indiscriminate destruction raging yet. There's only a little fighting, here and there, more suffering, more shouting.

Tom and I, we're still as close as fighting and there's hardly anything as close as that. I can see the appeal of conflict, feel how easy it is to get the taste for it. Underneath the shadow of our luck, we are still raw from fighting, tender and alight. I feel as if we could be naked.

We buy coffees with a credit card and sit outside, looking up at the mountain of cathedral and its two peaks. We argued in the left tower, or it may have been the right. We are incredibly hungry. We buy more coffee and slices of a cake. These are some of the many things we can do just because we'd like to. Lucky, lucky. Tiny, tiny.

We hold hands again. We had a fight and we survived it. The whole thing ended itself, almost without our help. Lucky, lucky. Tiny, tiny.

The afternoon is emptying and I want to ask Tom about what makes his hands shake sometimes, what his body is remembering. I want to know how he got the mark on his back, but it seems as if the words for that would make us filthy when we're still a little blessed. So instead I talk about the satellite they sent up, ages ago – we were practically children then – pushed it out into nowhere and let it shine. Tom remembers that it was called *Voyager*, which I remember, too – it's a nice name, suitable. *Voyager* must be so far by now and further each moment, deep out in the dark like an old idea with no returning.

To let outer space understand us, the satellite carried along information: birdsong and thunder and measurements and music and a message in languages. I've always remembered that part of the message said, *We are attempting to survive our time*. This seemed, to me, very brave and frail and hopeful.

Tom and I ought to be heading for our hotel – to the room we should give to a homeless person, because we can buy another and at least they'd be happy then for a night.

We delay, though, wander along the pedestrian precinct, the shop windows full of special offers.

Everywhere has sales now, all the time.

The homeless person thing would be too complicated – it's a thought we discuss to make ourselves feel kind, but we'll keep our room. We just won't enjoy it and we aren't going to make for it yet. We aren't quite going to be alone with each other inside it, aren't about to discover the way we will feel now, not for a while.

As we pass an open door we can hear voices, singing voices swimming out into the softening light. We go inside, do that together.

Beyond a tiny vestibule is a wide, low space set aside for performances of some kind, although there is no actual stage. People stand neatly in an arc, each dressed in various types of black clothing. The black is for their dignity, you can tell – and out of respect for the music, maybe – the music which is making them sound like bells. We will remember this. They are chiming like bells, being other than human and therefore remarkable, lovely.

A scattered audience is sitting on cheap plastic chairs and we settle ourselves in the back row. We will talk about this later – the time when we had the appalling row, the one that could have finished us, but then it didn't and then there was a choir and this sound which felt exactly how we felt. Reality seemed to turn round and look at us, give us this especially.

It made us lucky again, in a way that had no shadow.

The row of seats directly in front of us is empty, but a black backpack is resting on one of the chairs. It has no apparent owner.

I stare at it. Tom is staring too.

We live in a time when a bag with no owner can only hold terrible things.

In this moment, or this moment, or this moment we could be torn apart by flying horror.

Pipe bomb, nail bomb, Semtex, gelignite. I can say words from the languages of bombs, but I don't understand them. The films we watch are full up with explosions – so are our television shows, books, newspapers, magazines. It's as if we haven't had enough war, lately.

And the backpack leans against the seat and in this moment, or this moment, or this moment we could die.

That's always true, though. That was always true and always will be and needs no help – we could always die and are lucky not to. *We are attempting to survive our time.*

I may be sitting behind a bomb, Tom may be. We may die very soon and are no longer looking at the bomb, only at each other, and Tom's face is almost smiling and I am wondering why he's happy, much more than I am wondering what we should do.

I feel myself thinking that we are having a modern experience.

And then the music finishes with a desperate swoop of chimes and we clap – carefully, because of the backpack, which might be a bomb. Most probably it's safe and we're still lucky. Although we've been told that we ought to be fearful – angry and fearful – on every occasion – by our films, our television shows, books, newspapers, magazines – we've resisted it. We don't want every day of our adult lives to be like our childhoods.

One of the singers strolls towards the backpack, studies me, then picks it up. He is careless of tripwires, or mercury switches, pulls open the zip and tilts the bag's mouth towards us, shows us a range of CDs, neat inside.

He smiles.

I smile.

Tom smiles.

It's something to smile about – not dead yet.

We buy a CD.

Tomorrow we'll fly back to our little island. We don't know what will save us there. We'll want to save each other, be the saving of each other. We'll hope to be lucky, lucky enough.

Tiny, tiny. Gentle, gentle. Lucky, lucky.

We are attempting to survive our time.

Acknowledgements

PILLGWENLLY

The following stories have appeared in some form in other publications:

'Panic Attack' appeared in the anthology *A Short Affair*, Simon & Schuster, 2018

'Inappropriate Staring' appeared in the anthology *A Country of Refuge*, Unbound, 2016

'Am Sontag' appeared in the anthology *24 Stories*, Unbound, 2018

'Point For Lost Children' appeared in the anthology *Others*, Unbound, 2019